He lifted his hand and traced the silvered profile with one finger.

'I think you've knocked me senseless.'

Her eyes widened and a faint frown appeared between her eyebrows. His finger touched the tiny crease, smoothing at it as if to erase it.

'I'm sorry, I shouldn't have blurted that out but it seems to be the truth. And I don't know why you're looking puzzled. You're a beautiful woman. You must know the effect you have on men.'

'Not all men,' she said gravely. 'Not on men like you.'

Dear Reader

Doctors in the Outback, this series of four books set in the Australian Outback, of which OUTBACK ENCOUNTER is the third, was prompted by a big change in my own life. My husband and I shifted from a house on the very edge of Australia, overlooking a broad stretch of water that feeds in from the Pacific Ocean, to a small cottage in a small Outback town (population about 2,500) in Central Queensland. From the beach to the bush—that's an Aussie word for anywhere that isn't in a city.

After the rush and bustle of the tourist-oriented city where we lived before, the relaxed pace of the Outback really suits us. Where before we had jet-skis roaring past as we ate breakfast on the front deck, now we have a large and very quiet kangaroo occasionally popping in to feed on our well-watered back lawn, and the most dominant noise is birdsong.

I am really enjoying my new life in the Outback, and I hope these books will bring you a taste of it—a taste of the variety of life in the bush, the highs and lows, the tears and laughter, and, of course, the love those that live out here seek and find.

With best wishes

Meredith Webber

OUTBACK ENCOUNTER

BY
MEREDITH WEBBER

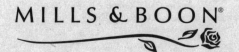

MILLS & BOON®

First published in Great Britain 2003
Harlequin Mills & Boon Limited,
Eton House, 18-24 Paradise Road, Richmond, Surrey TW9 1SR

© Meredith Webber 2003

ISBN 0 263 83877 3

Set in Times Roman 10½ on 11 pt.
03-0204-52935

Printed and bound in Spain
by Litografia Rosés, S.A., Barcelona

CHAPTER ONE

'CAITLIN O'SHEA? Wait till Mother hears I've a visitor with such a grand Irish name. She'll have wedding bells ringing for sure. Do you see this, Mrs Neil? I'm to provide all help and support to a Dr O'Shea by order of the government who pays both our wages.'

Connor ignored the tiny prick of fear the fax had caused and waved the flimsy piece of fax paper towards the woman who came in once a week to clean his house. He didn't pass it to her, being reasonably certain reading was one of the things Mrs Neil 'preferred not to do'. Instead, he read on.

'It says she'll be here four to six weeks—do you suppose that means I have to house her as well?' He spoke lightly, hoping the fear would dissipate if he pretended it wasn't there.

Mrs Neil continued to push the vacuum cleaner across the carpet square in the centre of the room she called the lounge. Talking was another thing she preferred not to do.

'Perhaps she could use that small house at the back of the hospital,' Connor continued, undeterred by both the one-sidedness of the conversation and his own unwelcome reaction—now fading to a vague uneasiness.

'That's Matron's house,' Mrs Neil objected, forced into speech to defend the proprieties.

'But Matron doesn't live there,' Connor pointed out. OK, so he'd overreacted to the thought of a new woman doctor in the town. Now all he had to contend with was regret that he'd felt the urge to force Mrs Neil into speech. Why couldn't he learn to let well alone, to allow Mrs Neil to come and go without a word spoken between them?

5

Actually, he knew why.

When he'd first arrived in Turalla two years earlier he'd been anxious and uncertain, hiding wounds he'd hoped the locals would never guess at. Mrs Neil had been introduced as one of the hospital staff he would be seeing on a regular basis so it had seemed natural to him to develop some kind of relationship with the woman. For a start, she'd known Angie.

Two years later, 'develop' seemed optimistic, the 'relationship' was still a dream, while Angie's name had never passed her lips. Yet every Tuesday morning he made the effort to be sociable. And every Tuesday morning was rebuffed.

He continued, 'Matron—' Mrs Neil hadn't moved with the times as far as staff titles were concerned '—lives in a house with four bedrooms and a pool on a hill on the edge of town, which is where I should live if I had a scrap of sense.'

He muttered the last sentence to himself as he walked back to the room he called his office. He had an official office at the hospital but, as every inhabitant of the town seemed to wander at will through the building, he'd taken to keeping most of his correspondence at home.

Home was an old wooden house built high to catch the breeze. Part of the hospital complex, it was a three-minute walk—across the parking lot and through a dried-out park, with paint-chipped swings and tired-looking acacia trees—from the main building.

It was no good suggesting Mrs Neil clean the vacant house in preparation for the visitor. Mrs Neil's chain of command began and ended with 'Matron', although how someone as set in her ways as his domestic help had accepted a male in this role, Connor often wondered.

Lifting the phone, he pressed the button that would put him through to Mike's office.

He explained the situation, received assurances that the house would be made ready for a visitor, then rebuffed

Mike's final comment with, 'No, Mike, I doubt she'll be blonde and shapely. When did I ever get that lucky?'

The shapely blonde was, at that very moment, forcing her gritty eyes to stay open and promising her sleep-deprived body it couldn't possibly be much further.

Both the blonde hair and the shapeliness were natural— a genetic curse, she'd decided when her effect on people had first become apparent. Women tended to label her a Barbie doll and steer clear of her company, while the word 'bimbo' seemed to hover in men's heads when they first met her. The image reduced their conversation to such mundane levels that she rarely bothered to reply, so had gained a reputation for aloofness—even rudeness. Pushy, too! But women had to be pushy to climb ladders usually reserved for men.

She sighed, hating the label as much as she hated the politics and infighting in the money-starved research unit where she held her precarious tenure.

'Another thirty minutes, and there'll be a hot shower and a real bed somewhere in Turalla. If the hospital can't provide them I'll book into a motel.'

It was a pledge she'd been making to herself for the past five hundred kilometres. Ever since she'd repacked her overnight gear at three-thirty this morning and stormed out of the hotel next to the cattle yards where the mournful lowing of the unhappy beasts had added a deep counterpoint to a train engine shunting back and forth beyond her window.

At five, she'd refuelled at a truck stop, intending to grab a cup of coffee and some food. Suggestive remarks from the all-male clientele had moved her on without the food and drink, so now the end of her journey was taking on mythical proportions—the thought of that shower and a comfortable bed luring her on as surely as the sirens' songs had lured sailors onto rocks.

But Turalla was in the outback—no rocks…

She drove with a fierce concentration, aware that the tree-covered hills had given way to plains—endless miles of emptiness stretching to a far horizon. Cattle country, she reminded herself, and wondered where the cotton was grown. Perhaps the other side of the town?

The little she knew about Turalla, a medley of ill-assorted facts, swirled in her head like leaves in a willy-willy. Old gold-mining town, huge open-cut coal mine nearby, cotton-growing begun when the river had been dammed and water had become available for irrigation.

Cancer cluster.

Cancer clusters happened, she reminded herself. They were an inexplicable phenomenon but common enough to be written up in any number of medical texts.

Other experts had been to Turalla and decided the cases weren't linked by any discoverable cause. Would she find any clues?

The question raised a new spark of energy and she straightened behind the wheel.

Sure, she would! She was a woman and women could do *anything*.

She repeated the words that were her personal mantra, then sang them, slightly off-key, while she tapped out a rap beat on the steering wheel.

Tall silos appeared in the distance—deceptively close. Perhaps another twenty minutes before she actually drove through their elongated shadows but they signalled the end of her journey. With the new energy flowing, she looked across the plains, her thoughts leaping ahead.

Hospital first—meet this Dr Clarke and find out about accommodation. She'd explain later why she'd come—if no one had already filled him in.

She passed the silos standing guard over the railway tracks and saw the sign to the hospital. Swinging left, she drove more slowly down the wide street, studded with houses on one side and emptiness on the other. She knew enough about country towns to recognise the design. Out here, habitation ended abruptly—not dwindling into a scattering of houses and businesses as cities did. It was as if someone had drawn a line. On one side of the outermost road was 'the town'—however small the settlement, it still clung to township—and on the other side 'the bush'.

The hospital was instantly recognisable, a low-set wooden building surrounded by wide verandas with various outbuildings strewn behind and to the side of it. A thin spiral of smoke drifted from the tall chimney of the incinerator. It looked white against the fierce blue of the sky and seemed to hang above the hospital like a benevolent spirit. Well, hopefully benevolent!

Caitlin parked her car in front of the main building and carefully eased her cramped and aching body out of its confinement. As she stretched she looked around but her mind was too numb from lack of sleep to take in much of her surroundings. The burst of energy had fizzled out, leaving her drained and empty.

Shower and bed, she reminded herself, hoping the magic words would give her the strength to climb the three steps up onto the veranda. She clicked the automatic lock on the car doors and headed purposefully towards the building.

A wide hall opened off the veranda and the first door on the left bore a neatly printed 'Of ice' label. Some wit had scribbled over the second 'f' and written 'out' above the word but it was close enough for Caitlin. She knocked, then pushed the door open as a male voice called to her to enter.

'I'm Caitlin O'Shea,' she began, holding out her hand to the man who had risen to his feet behind a cluttered desk.

He recognised the name and she recognised his reaction. The incredulous question 'You're a doctor?' was all but tattooed across his forehead.

He stretched out his hand and managed to mumble

something appropriate about pleasure and welcome, then added 'Sorry we didn't have a bet?' in an aside to someone else.

Caitlin turned to find a second man in the room. The open door had hidden him from view, but he was definitely there. A tall, rangy-looking man with softly curling reddish-brown hair, round-rimmed glasses and a smile she'd have to consider later—when she wasn't feeling like a bit of chewed string. He had one denim-clad hip hitched up on a table but he levered himself to his feet, took off his glasses and shoved them into the pocket of his pale blue shirt, then he, too, stretched out his hand.

'Connor Clarke,' he said, and she gave him full marks for making and maintaining eye contact. 'I'm the doctor in charge at Turalla and this is Mike Nelson, our director of nursing. I had a fax this morning to say you were coming, but it failed to mention when. Mike and I were just discussing accommodation for you. There's a small house behind the main building you could use, if you haven't made other arrangements.'

His voice was deliberately neutral—but he couldn't conceal the gleam of humour lurking in his eyes. Something to do with the bet?

She allowed herself a small smile in response to that gleam.

'As long as it's got hot water and a bed, it'll be fine,' she told him. 'I spent part of the night in the hotel from hell—about six hundred kilometres back down the road—'

'Calthorpe!' the two men chorused.

'Cattle sales today,' Mike explained. 'Did you have the train or just the cattle?'

'Both,' Caitlin admitted, feeling her body relax and her smile widen. 'If it's a weekly event there should be a sign outside the town telling unwary travellers to drive straight through on Mondays.'

Connor watched the smile drive the greyness of fatigue

from her face and felt a twinge of something he barely recognised as attraction. She was certainly beautiful enough to attract any man's attention. Clear smooth skin, golden hair, dark eyes above moulded cheekbones, lips that could… He caught his wayward thoughts and hauled them back under control.

'If you've driven from there this morning, you're over-due for some sleep,' he said. 'Where's your car? Your gear? I came over to ask Mike to have the house cleaned, but you can take a shower then crash at my place while that's being done. Your introduction to your new home sweet home will wait. Come on, I'll take you across.'

She hesitated, as if obeying orders didn't sit easily on her lovely shoulders, then she dipped her head, said 'See you later' to Mike, and allowed Connor to usher her out the door.

The bright red, low-slung Porsche parked outside made him groan. It was just too trite—this 'blonde in the red sports car' image.

'Well, you'll sure make a splash in this town!' he said, and felt his companion stiffen. Wrong move, Clarke, he told himself. Could be a while before she smiles at you again.

He heard the noise of the alarm and door locks deactivating and strove to make amends.

'I'll take your bag for you. It's quicker to walk across to my place, but if you'll trust me with the keys I'll put the car under cover for you once I've shown you around.'

She swung to face him, the smile back in place.

'Want to drive it, don't you?' she teased, and he found himself nodding as he smiled foolishly back at her. 'It's my one rebellion,' she added, leaning into the back seat and pulling out a duffel bag. 'One thing in my life that's not constrained by the narrow boundaries of the known.'

She shouldered the bag and tossed the keys to him.

'Dent it and I'll kill you. Now, lead me to the bath-room.'

He decided he'd look foolish offering to carry her bag for a second time, so he waved his hand for her to follow and headed off across the asphalt car park, past the swings and through the opening in the fence that led into his yard. Covering familiar ground made unfamiliar by company. He tried to see the place through her eyes, to analyse the old timber structure he now called home.

But all he noticed was how badly it needed painting.

'We've a crew of painters due in a couple of weeks—they'll do the hospital and all the outbuildings, this one included.'

He explained this as they climbed the steps, breaking a slightly daunting silence that had strained the air between them.

'Here's the kitchen. Laundry and bathroom through there and to the left of the bathroom, if you walk out onto the veranda, you'll find a spare bedroom. There are towels in a cupboard in the laundry. Why don't you have a shower while I throw clean sheets on the bed?'

She didn't answer, seemingly more interested in examining his kitchen than in the shower she'd wanted earlier. She dropped her bag and looked around.

'Do you cook?' she asked when her survey was completed.

'Not well enough to justify all this gear,' he admitted, waving a hand to where an amazing array of stainless-steel implements hung from an old cartwheel suspended above an island bench. 'I inherited them from the previous occupant. I guess the local charity shop knew the townspeople well enough to know they wouldn't sell, so whoever cleaned out the house left the kitchen as it was.'

Tired as she was, Caitlin heard the constraint in his voice. What had happened to the previous occupant that a 'whoever' had cleaned out the house?

'Shower's that way,' her guide repeated, cutting off any question she might have been tempted to ask. 'Unlimited hot water so take your time. Would you like a cup of tea or coffee when you finish? I can put the kettle on when I hear the shower go off.'

Was he real, this lean, casual guy making such sensible suggestions?

'I'd probably sell my soul for a cup of tea,' she told him. 'That's if I haven't already mortgaged it for the shower.'

She smiled at him and was pleased to see him smile back. Maybe it was exhaustion muddling her mind, but it seemed important he should like her.

Connor watched the bathroom door close behind her and sighed. No matter how blonde and shapely she was, she was only passing through his life, he reminded himself, but he whistled quietly as he found clean sheets, and wondered if he should check the old matron's house for wood-rot or lice—find some excuse to have the visitor stay on in his spare bedroom.

'You've been too long on your own, Connor, lad,' he muttered in a fair imitation of his mother's tones. His mother usually added 'Time you found yourself a nice girl and settled down', but would the beauty in the red sports car meet his mother's idea of 'nice'?

Angie had.

But, then, Angie had been everyone's idea of nice.

Images he'd thought he'd buried long ago recurred, the wedge of fear returning to dig into his ribs, while the question hammered once again in his head.

Why had Angie died?

It was an accident, he repeated to himself for the four-thousandth time. He tucked the sheets under the foot of the bed and squared the corners as the aides in the hospital did each morning.

It *had* to have been an accident.

Would it have happened if he'd given in and chosen to work in the country with her? Could he have kept her safe or was death—and therefore life—pre-ordained?

And if so, had pre-ordination brought him Caitlin O'Shea?

He stopped what he was doing and stared out through the open door. Neither he nor Mike had thought to ask her why she'd come to Turalla. Hadn't thought of much at all, in fact, simply letting their libidos run a little wild and surreptitiously examining the waving golden blonde hair and lush, luscious body only partially hidden by jeans and a faded chambray shirt not unlike the one he was wearing himself.

No, Mike probably hadn't done that at all. Mike had Sue at home to keep his libido happy.

Banishing the distracting images of the visitor, he pulled a light cotton coverlet up over the sheets then realised the water had stopped running in the bathroom. He'd promised her tea—he'd better get moving.

Caitlin wrapped a towel, turban-style, around her wet hair and dried her body with another. It was then she remembered she'd dropped her bag on the kitchen floor.

A slightly faded towelling robe hung on a hook behind the bathroom door so, with a silent apology to her host, she snagged it down and pulled it on. It had a strangely masculine scent to it—not unpleasant, in fact quite comforting—evoking memories of herself as a small child, climbing on her father's knee for her goodnight story.

She considered using her host's comb to untangle her hair but decided that would be taking too much advantage of his hospitality. The tangles would have to stay in place.

Collecting her dirty clothes in one hand, she opened the door and headed back towards the kitchen. He was over by a bench beneath the window, pouring water into the teapot. Her reaction to this back view of the man made her wonder if there was a Mrs Clarke.

'I forgot to take my clothes through to the bathroom so I borrowed your robe. I hope you don't mind.' The words came tumbling out, talking to hide her embarrassment at her own unruly thoughts.

'Mind?' Connor turned as he spoke, then he smiled again. 'How could I possibly mind when you make it look so good? I'd been thinking I should get a new one but that old thing has suddenly taken on a whole new lease of life.'

He set the teapot on a small table by a second window.

'Here you go. I've toast cooking—it's what I'm good at, toast—or I've biscuits and a bit of slightly suspicious-looking fruit cake. I've examined it for mould but it looks OK. Patients give me these things but they never put a ''use by'' date on them.'

He waved her towards the table, pointing out the un-inspiring view of the hospital it afforded. Caitlin obeyed the gesture, wondering if he, too, was a little uneasy in this situation. Or did he talk non-stop all the time?

'Toast! Sorry there's no silver toast rack to keep it crisp.'

He pushed a plate with two golden toasted slices of bread towards her.

'The previous occupant not into toast?' she asked lightly, and was surprised to see a shadow darken his eyes before he turned away to brush crumbs from the bench.

Nice eyes they were, too—even darkened by that shadow. A kind of greenish blue, like deep creek water on a hot day.

'The previous occupant died,' he said, and all thoughts of eyes—nice or not—were forgotten.

'The doctor who was here before you died? I'm presuming this is a hospital house?'

He nodded in reply to one or both Caitlin's questions, and shifted so he could hitch his hip onto the bench.

'Do you know much about Turalla?' he asked, the switch in conversation so obvious Caitlin wondered why the subject of his predecessor was taboo. Well, she was new here and had to learn as much as possible so she'd play along with him.

'Small town, originally founded in a gold rush. When

most of the miners moved on to the next bonanza, some people took up land in the area and stayed on to farm so a small section of the original town survived to serve the farmers. Later, rich coal deposits brought in a huge mining operation and today about a quarter of the population work in jobs connected with the mine.'

She spread marmalade on her toast as she spoke and cut it into neat squares as he replied.

'You've done your homework. Did it cover cotton?'

He snapped the question at her and she tried a smile to dispel a feeling of uneasiness. 'Do I win a prize if I get all the answers right?'

He shook his head and the sunlight from the window turned his hair to a halo of reddish brown.

'I'm sorry. I guess I've been here too long! I've developed small-town syndrome.'

'Which is?'

'Suspicion of any newcomer. Oh, we get plenty of visitors coming through the town. People come to fossick around the old goldfields, but they usually stay in the caravan park and I don't get introductory faxes about them.'

Connor had the contrite look of a small boy caught out in mischief so it was easy to accept the apology. He was right about small towns but she'd have said the syndrome was revealed in curiosity rather than suspicion. She filed the word away in her mind and decided to tread more warily.

'I do know about the cotton,' she said. 'And the dam, and the problems over irrigation rights—and the cancer cluster.'

The final words dropped into the warm air like pebbles into a pond. Caitlin could almost feel their ripples spreading outward.

'Cancer clusters happen,' he said flatly, a defensive shield springing up between them. 'They occur time and time again in communities all over the world and are sheer coincidence. It was before my arrival in Turalla but I do know what went on up here. After some totally insensitive journalist broke a highly emotive TV story about the place, the Health Department sent up every kind of expert to try to establish links. They tested all the farm and mine chemicals, tested air and water, dissected locally grown meat and vegetables, and came up with a big fat zero.'

'You're very defensive for someone who wasn't here,' she suggested, and watched him shrug as if to ease his tension. The marmalade was homemade, sweet and tart at once—a kind of metaphor for this man…

'It's that syndrome again,' he said, but although she waited for a smile it didn't come. 'I've only been here two years but already the town feels like my town, the people I treat my friends. Because the original focus was medical, the hospital was at the centre of things—still is in some ways. The four surviving children are my patients, and while the kids are all in remission now, some close to being what we'd call cured, their parents carry the fear of recurrence or of a sibling being affected.'

Shifting from the bench, he came towards her, ran his fingers through his hair, sighed, then sat down at the table opposite her. Caitlin felt his tension as if he carried it in a force-field around his body. She chose another square of toast and bit into it, knowing he had more to say and prepared to wait until he was ready to say it.

'When the first child was diagnosed, the medical emergency united the town—everyone dug in to help. When another child fell ill, then another followed, it was as if the town had rehearsed their parts. Because treatment was only available in the city, the townspeople raised money for the parents to accompany the children. Neighbours minded the siblings and the service clubs organised special events for them to distract them from the upheaval in their young lives.'

'You know all this although you weren't here?'

He shifted in the chair, as if the question was a missile he might dodge.

'Like any halfway competent practitioner, I need to know the history of the patient before I can attempt a diagnosis. I made it my business to find out. Not that it was difficult. Most patients are only too anxious to tell their side of things.'

The explanation sounded reasonable, but Caitlin sensed evasiveness behind the words. Did resentment remain although it had been years since the other scientists had arrived to conduct their tests? And if so, how would that affect her work?

'Why did the scientific investigation cause problems?' she persisted, pushing aside the now empty plate and pouring herself another cup of tea. 'Why didn't the townspeople welcome the chance to find out what was happening?'

'It's probably hard for someone looking in from the outside to understand, but the arrival of those so-called experts caused huge divisions in this town. Everybody had a pet theory. The "old" locals blamed the mine, the cattle people blamed the chemicals used on the cotton crops, brawls broke out in pubs and shots were fired from cars. This town went from a place united by the illness of a handful of its children to a virtual war zone.'

'But surely the ill feeling must have been there all along, hidden beneath the surface. The testing may have provided a focus, which would explain why the violence erupted so suddenly.'

'Like someone lighting a fuse already in place? You could be right,' he admitted, twirling the teapot around in circles and watching the movement as if it absorbed all his attention. 'I know the cattle men had resented the irrigation rights given to the cotton growers and there's been a historical division between the miners and the primary producers, but it had been a niggling kind of enmity—not an explosive force.'

Connor paused, looking up at Caitlin, then bending his

head again as if the words he wanted were written on the table.

'It might have happened years ago, but the animosities still linger.'

'And the hospital?' Caitlin asked. 'Where do you sit?'

'Slap bang in the middle of it. There's a little thing called the Hippocratic oath to deal with—service to all people. Besides, I'm the only doctor in town, so they have to be nice to me. Trouble is—'

'You hear both sides of the story.'

He glanced up at her, as if startled by her perception, and she smiled at him.

'I'm not totally insensitive to the dynamics of small-town life,' she said. 'In fact, if you're city-born I probably understand them better than you do. Try as I do to forget it, I grew up in a town like Turalla. My father was the local doctor. The hospital, the house—even the tatty park and swings—are all eerily familiar. It's a bit like coming home—or perhaps going back in time. When I was younger, all I ever wanted to do was get out of the place, to hit the city where I could be anonymous, a no one, not "the doctor's daughter".'

Connor studied her across the table. Even in his far from glamorous bathrobe and with her lovely hair hidden in a hospital-issue towel, she was like an exotic orchid transplanted into the drabness of his surroundings.

'Anonymous?' he teased, raising one eyebrow but smiling to ward off any offence. 'Like supermodels are anonymous?'

'Believe me, at sixteen, when I went down to the city to finish my schooling, I didn't look like this. Zits and braces, hair in a long thick plait down my back—the duckling showed absolutely no sign of becoming a swan.'

'And when it happened?'

It was her turn to sigh.

'I was in med school and it was a darned nuisance. All I wanted to do was study, to learn as much as I could. I loved it, loved the challenge of the work, the science of it all. I was fascinated by the exactness of mathematics, by microscopes and slides. Then suddenly there were boys I'd known for ages panting over me, as if having breasts had suddenly transformed me from one of the guys to a sex object. Believe me, it's no fun. They even talked differently to me. Remember all the blonde jokes? I actually had people explaining them to me!'

Connor found himself chuckling at her disgust, yet he was pleased to hear her speak so matter-of-factly about her appearance. No pride, but no false modesty either. She'd accepted the transformation to swan, though she might chafe against the burden that came with it.

'I must be keeping you from your work,' she said, switching the conversation away from herself. 'Don't feel you have to entertain me.'

'It's Tuesday. I've done a morning ward round and usually do minor operations on Tuesday mornings, but for once there wasn't anyone who required my cutting or stitching expertise so I've nothing on my schedule until this afternoon's clinic. But don't let me keep you talking. You wanted to catch up on your sleep.'

Caitlin smiled at him and lifted one hand to tug the towel from around her wet hair.

'I was so tired I thought I'd sleep for a week,' she admitted, 'but the shower seems to have woken me up.'

She combed her fingers through the damp strands, as unselfconscious as a child. Wet, her hair seemed darker, almost brown, the same colour as her eyebrows, and the soft fan of lashes framing her dark eyes.

Should he ask her why she was here?

Of course he should.

So why was he hesitating?

Caitlin sensed his hesitation. She tracked back through the conversation to where he'd shifted it sideways with talk of the town and the fallout from the TV report.

'How did your predecessor die? From the way you spoke, it was unexpected. An accident?'

The wall came up between them once again, but she refused to break the silence and finally he spoke again.

'Yes!'

Silence returned.

'Vehicle?'

He raised his head and looked at her, studying her face as if trying to fathom her interest—or her willingness to persist until she had an answer. He must have read something in her eyes, for he ran his fingers through his hair again, lifted his shoulders in a heavy shrug, then replied.

'She fell down a mine shaft.'

The words were rough-edged, scything through the air like a too-blunt knife through bread, shedding tatters of emotion like crumbs.

'Here at Turalla? I thought the mine was an open-cut operation. I didn't realise there were shafts.'

He shook his head then propped his elbows on the table and lowered his head to his hands. Not looking at her this time, he repeated words that must have figured in some report, so concisely did he recite them.

'It is assumed the deceased was walking through the bush when she saw the old mine shaft.' He glanced up again, explaining, 'We're talking old gold mines here, not the coal mine.'

Caitlin nodded, her mind racing as she tried to work out why this man had taken his predecessor's death so personally. Before she could ask, he bent his head once more and finished his recital, the words delivered without intonation, flat and hard and cold as a steel blade.

'Perhaps moving closer to investigate the excavation, it appears the deceased slipped. The depth of the shaft, when measured, was seventy-two feet, so death was probably instantaneous.'

'Probably instantaneous?' Caitlin repeated. 'Surely the medical examiner could do better than "probably".'

'Not after sixteen months.' Connor lifted his head and she saw the pain in his eyes. *He'd* been the medical examiner. *He'd* been the one who'd had to prod and pry and poke at that broken body.

'Sixteen months—that's a long time for her family and friends to have lived without knowing what happened to her.'

Her host nodded grimly.

'It was only sheer luck she was found then. Some of the professional gold-seekers have started detecting the walls of old mines. They use slings and ropes and pulleys—and are quite safe as long as they keep an eye out for snakes that get down into the shafts. They've found the bones of cattle in holes and the occasional kangaroo, but kangaroos don't wear wristwatches. She was identified by the jewellery she was wearing.'

Something in this blunt presentation of facts chilled Caitlin's blood and she shivered in the warm air.

'When did it happen?' she asked, sorry she'd brought up the subject but unable to let it die now she knew the stark outline of the story.

'She went missing right in the middle of the leukaemia war. In fact, if the hospital and medical staff hadn't remained so determinedly neutral throughout all the mud-slinging and finger-pointing, I imagine her disappearance would have attracted a lot more attention.'

An added chill produced goose bumps, making the hairs on Caitlin's arms stand to attention. Rubbing her hands across her skin, she stared at the man across the table, willing him to lift his head and look at her before she asked the next question.

Connor felt her attention focussing on him like a laser beam. He banished thoughts of Angie and raised his head, blinking his eyes at the extravagant beauty of this woman who had lobbed into his life as unexpectedly as a mishit tennis ball into a football game.

'You said "attention" but the word sounded more like "suspicion". You don't think it was an accident.'

Statements, not questions. He didn't have to answer statements. But her curiosity should be dispelled before she started to dig deeper into what he thought or didn't think about the situation.

'As I said, I wasn't here when it happened. I've no reason to think it was anything other than an accident. Believe me, tempers were running so high at the time I'm sure if there'd been the slightest whiff of suspicion someone would have said something. Apparently she liked to walk in the bush when she was off duty. She collected rocks and fossils. The stones are still here in the house somewhere. No, it was an accident.'

Or you want me to believe it was, Caitlin decided, stacking her cup and saucer on the dirty plate and standing up to take the crockery over to the sink.

'I think I will have that sleep,' she said, 'but perhaps the house is ready now. I could go over there.'

Connor rose to his feet and reached out to take the dirty dishes out of her hands.

'Mrs Neil isn't one to vary her routine. She'll finish at the hospital at precisely two o'clock, then start on the house. You're welcome to use my spare bedroom. I'll help you get settled into your temporary home when I finish my afternoon session.'

How's that for a dismissal? Caitlin thought as she grabbed her bag and headed through the laundry and bathroom to the veranda, turned left as directed and entered the bedroom through open French doors.

And why hadn't he asked her why she was here?

The question made her frown for the two seconds it took to pull back the coverlet and collapse onto the bed, but her last hazy thought as she drifted off to sleep was about the man himself, not the question he hadn't asked. Were his eyes greenish blue or bluey green?

CHAPTER TWO

CAITLIN woke with a feeling of disorientation. The room was dark and shadowy, and she had a sense someone had watched her as she slept. Clutching her host's bathrobe about her body, she stepped quietly out to the veranda and looked around.

The day had all but disappeared, leaving a wash of brilliant colour across the western sky, while the stillness dusk brought in its wake seemed to hover over the hospital complex. She listened but could hear nothing beyond the occasional growl of a car engine on a distant street and the hum of an air-conditioning plant—presumably over at the main building. Was Connor still working?

Connor. The name curled around her tongue and she allowed it to float softly from her lips. Perhaps he'd looked in to see if she was awake—that would explain the feeling of another presence in the room.

Either that or his predecessor's ghost, Caitlin joked to herself as she went back into the bedroom to find clean clothes. She'd have another shower, wash away these fancies, then tidy herself up and go across to her temporary quarters. The sooner she was unpacked and could get down to work the better.

He was home by the time she emerged, for a light was on in the kitchen and the sounds of a string quartet drifted through the air.

'Feeling better?' he asked as she came into the big room and once again dropped her bag on the floor. There was no string quartet in evidence, but an elaborate stereo set-up on a shelf against the far wall suggested he used this room more than any other.

24

'One hundred per cent,' she assured him, her gaze drawn again to his eyes—but only to check their colour. 'If you point me towards my home, I'll go over and settle in.'

'I'll feed you first,' he offered. 'You can usually scrounge a meal in the hospital kitchen but it's getting late and Nellie will be packing up for the night. As well as toast, I do a mean steak and salad if you're prepared to risk it.'

She hesitated, knowing it was a sensible suggestion. They also had to discuss the reason for her visit to Turalla—the one subject they'd managed to avoid earlier in the day. Yet instinct told her spending too much time with Connor Clarke might prove unsettling—even dangerous.

Nonsense, her sane inner self retorted.

'If you let me help,' she said aloud, mentally crossing her fingers and hoping the inner self was right. 'I'm a dab hand at washing lettuce.' ·

Connor reached into the refrigerator and pulled out a lettuce. He set it down on the bench then stepped away. Images of his visitor had floated in his mind all afternoon, distracting him as he'd dealt with patients and prescribed medication to ease their aches and illnesses.

Now the real thing was back in his kitchen, lovelier than his images, making faded blue jeans and an overlarge white shirt look elegant and sexy at the same time, her long blonde hair shimmering to her shoulder blades like an ad for a shampoo commercial.

He could understand the poor guys who'd explained the blonde jokes. It seemed incredible to a male mind that brains could come in such a stunning package.

'I asked if you had a bowl.'

He stared at her, trying to compute the words. Pity he hadn't a few more grey cells himself to replace the ones she'd knocked askew. He was the least sexist man he knew, so why was he standing in his own kitchen thinking such sexist thoughts?

'Yes, under that bench. Drawers pull out and there's an assortment of sizes. I've got some sprouts and tomatoes and other salad stuff in the refrigerator.' He paused, then added, 'I usually eat on the veranda. There's a table out there near the barbecue.'

It wasn't what he'd wanted to say but it filled the silence, and when he carried the plate of steak and sliced onions out on to the open area beyond the kitchen, she followed him.

'Country air always smells so clean,' she murmured, setting the salad bowl on the table and leaning out across the railing as if to take in more air than the house could offer. 'And verandas right around the house—I love the openness of it.'

'So the city that lured you at sixteen didn't steal your heart?' he asked, and she shook her head, blonde hair shimmering as light from the lamp reflected off it.

'No,' she said slowly. 'But what I found in the city did. Science stole my heart—permutations and combinations and searching for answers.'

Connor felt coldness settle in his stomach well before he asked the question, but it had to be asked. Should have been asked earlier.

He held his hand above the barbecue plate to test the heat, then threw the onions on to sizzle so the noise provided a background when he did say the words.

'And is that why you're here? Searching for answers?'

Caitlin didn't respond immediately and the coldness grew, sending icy shards through his veins, pricking and cutting at the flesh inside him.

'Looking more at permutations and combinations,' she said at last. 'I think answers are still a long way off.'

He dropped the steaks onto the grill and flipped the onions, concealing the rage and despair jostling for supremacy in his mind.

'I don't suppose it's anything other than the incidence of leukaemia that interests you?' he asked, his voice as cold as the blood within him.

He'd expected her to defend herself so when she didn't reply he continued.

'Look, this town has suffered enough. It's just getting over the divisions caused by the last round of experts. How do you think they're going to feel about you coming and poking your admittedly beautiful nose into their business?'

The anger remained but the despair had turned to the nameless kind of fear he'd felt earlier—not for himself, or the town, but for the woman who was about to stir up old animosities. He turned the steak then looked across to where she was standing, propped against the railing.

'Perhaps we could discuss this rationally,' she suggested bluntly. 'Leaving out all the emotive stuff about the town and divisions and considering one basic fact. It is only through continuing research that puzzles like leukaemia—any cancer, in fact—will eventually be solved.'

'You can't leave people out of the equation,' he objected, slapping steak and onions onto a plate and dumping it on the table. 'Researchers sitting in labs might be dealing with bundles of mutating cells but those cells came from living human beings who hurt and cry and feel the pain of others.'

He headed for the kitchen, grabbed cutlery and returned, anger still burning.

'What do you hope to find that the other so-called experts failed to discover? There's been no new case of leukaemia in this town for three and a half, nearly four, years. What can you possibly do at this stage?'

Caitlin felt the force of his anger but kept a clamp on her own temper. She understood what fuelled his rage but why were scientists always the bad guys? Why were they seen as passionless, unemotional people not affected by the pain and tears of others?

She sat down at the table and helped herself to salad, then, choosing her words carefully, said, 'The other experts tested external factors—water, soil, air—seeking something that may have caused the problem. I'm not here to look into possible causes, but to try to trace genetic links between the families.'

'Leukaemia as an inherited predisposition? I thought the latest research on leukaemia was centred on the possibility of viral causes.'

He joined her at the table, glaring across it as he rebutted her statement.

She nodded, glad he was up on the latest research.

'A virus that causes leukaemia in mice has been discovered, and an enormous amount of work is being carried out based on this find. No actual human virus has been isolated as yet, although the animal work points to the possibility of it. At the moment, scientists are studying a number of suspect viral infections which could be linked to cancer.'

'Can I hear a "but" hovering at the end of that sentence?'

A lightening of his voice told her he was calming down, perhaps even becoming interested. She tried some steak while she formulated an answer that wouldn't set up more barriers, and found it melting in her mouth. It was all she could do to stop the whimper of sheer pleasure.

'This is delicious—beautiful meat. I'd forgotten how good real food could be.'

Obviously startled by her statement, Connor lifted his head and studied her closely, eyes bright with disbelief.

'You don't eat real food?'

She grinned at his astonishment.

'Not for the last month or so. Once this project was mooted, I had to finish what I was working on and also do an enormous amount of preparatory work, not only searching out all the latest papers that might help but boning up on the history of each patient. I've lived on takeaways delivered to the lab, and breakfast cereal on the rare occasions I was home.'

He smiled and she felt her body relax, the tension generated earlier melting away. Mind you, it wasn't so surprising, the man had the kind of smile that would melt metal. The thought was so unexpected she found her cheeks grow warm and determinedly turned her attention from his smile and back to her dinner.

'Patient histories?' he repeated. 'Is that where the "but" comes in?'

'You're not an easy man to divert, are you?' she said. 'And as I'm eating your food, I guess I have to answer.'

She put down her fork and leaned forward across the table, using the clean tip of the knife to draw squiggles on the tablecloth as she spoke.

'With the virus that's been isolated, researchers haven't been able to transmit it from one animal to another through normal procedures like physical contact or air transmission.' She paused and looked up from her squiggles, wanting to see his reaction as she continued. 'With the lab mice, it's transmitted vertically through families, Connor, though not inevitably. Sometimes it passes from one infected female to one or all of her embryos at a very early stage in their development yet at other times the offspring are not affected.'

His dark eyebrows drew together in a puzzled frown.

'But what about siblings?' he demanded. 'Surely if it was passed down from parent to child all the children in the family would suffer and that doesn't happen.'

'We've known for some time there's a higher statistical likelihood of a twin contracting the disease, but the fact that some do and some don't, as with the mice, seems to suggest that, while there must be a degree of genetic involvement, the virus is only one of a number of things leading to malignancy.'

'So?' he asked, and she felt his hostility returning, although he was continuing to eat his meal as if unfazed by her words. She watched him for a moment, wanting to connect with the man on a friendly basis yet knowing it might not be possible, given his antagonism to her presence in the town and the job she was here to do.

'One way we might be able to take the research further—and translate it from the animals to humans—is through retrospective research.' The words sounded weak in her own ears. She tackled the salad, deciding the sooner she finished eating, the sooner she could get out of his house. Maybe when he'd had time to think things through…

'Looking back at people who've had or still have the disease?'

Caitlin nodded. 'That's right. And seeking possible links between them. You know how science works. You build up a theory then proceed to shoot it down.'

He actually paused in his eating as if this might be worth considering, but when he spoke she realised he'd only been gathering ammunition for another attack.

'But there must be other places in the world where leukaemia victims have been grouped in one area. In fact, I know there are. And other types of cancer in clusters. It's a well-known occurrence, although in many instances inexplicable. So why Turalla?'

She tried another smile but it was a strain.

'In places like Hiroshima after the war and Chernobyl after the nuclear explosion there were explainable incidences—radioactive contamination of both air and water—but to find new leads, science has to look for answers in the clusters where no contamination has been found—in towns like Turalla.'

Silence! A lack of response that went on so long Caitlin felt her own anger build. Once again she reined it in, though not tightly enough to stop having a small shot at him.

'It's the old Nimby attitude, isn't it? Not in my back

yard. Everyone would like an answer but don't let the research affect my town.'

'Hell!' he muttered, and stood up, pushing back his chair so quickly it tumbled over. By the time he'd picked it up, he seemed calmer.

'It's not that at all. I know what you're saying, and I understand the need for research, but haven't these families been through enough? Haven't studies been done elsewhere that could be related to this particular area without dragging these families into it?'

She watched Connor pace up and down beside the railing. He moved with the fluid grace of a big cat and once again she was touched by a shiver of some prescience she didn't understand. She couldn't match him for strength and wasn't about to react to his anger. Use the facts, her old professor had stated over and over again, not emotional arguments.

'Work has been done on what might be considered familial cancer in two strains of the disease, one prevalent in Africa and one in China. Both forms appear to be transmitted by a virus similar to the glandular fever virus. Scientists are trying to explain why some family members who contract the virus escape the cancer and others don't. That's the closest to what I want to study here.'

He stopped his pacing, as if struck by a winning argument.

'But what can you do here if no virus linked to leukaemia has been isolated as yet?'

'I can study the genetic make-up of all the members of the families involved, and eliminate the similarities. What's left will be the differences and perhaps, even without a virus, those differences will tell us something.'

Caitlin watched as he digested this information. Not a man to give in easily, she decided. Where would he attack from next?

'Do you realise not all the children had the same type of leukaemia? As I said, I wasn't here at the time, but from what I can remember of their files, there were different diagnoses.'

Conceding his point with a nod of her head, she gestured to his chair. Although the thought of beating a hasty retreat was appealing, it would be better if they could sort out their problems now. To achieve any measure of success she needed this man's support. Without it, she doubted she'd get much co-operation from the families concerned. It was time to try conciliation.

'Look, we have to thrash this out between us. What if I make coffee and we sit down and talk it through?'

'I'll make coffee,' he said gruffly, and disappeared through the door into the kitchen.

Caitlin collected up their plates and followed him.

'Go and sit down,' he said, shooing her out of the kitchen with a wave of one hand. 'I'll do the dishes later.'

Dismissed, she walked back onto the veranda. The moon had risen while they'd been eating and now hung, suspended, like a misshapen Chinese lantern set in the branches of the peppercorn tree.

A faint scent of eucalyptus filtered through the air, and somewhere an owl cried as it journeyed through the night in search of food. For all her haste to get away from her own home town, she felt the special ambience of a small country town settle about her. The unchanging rhythms of daily living far removed from the stress and pressures of the city were like a benediction on her soul.

'They have a special kind of innocence, country towns,' he said, as he returned with a coffee-pot in one hand and two tall mugs dangling from one finger of the other.

'You stole my thoughts,' she murmured.

The serenity of the evening seemed to envelop her, but it couldn't last, any more than innocence could—not in the face of evil or a hidden scourge like cancer.

Connor set down the pot and mugs.

'Milk or sugar?'

'No, thanks, just plain black,' she said, returning to the

table and waiting while he poured the coffee. Standing close to him like this, she realised he was taller than she'd thought. The top of her head was five feet eight inches from floor level, yet he stretched at least six inches beyond that.

And solid height, well muscled by the look of the tautness of shirt across his torso, good strong neck—

'OK—so talk!' he said, moving to sit back down in his chair and waving her to the other side of the table.

Caitlin took her seat and sipped at her coffee, trying to gather thoughts that had strayed too far. For heaven's sake! She'd been examining the man like a buyer at a cattle sale might examine a likely beast! What had they been discussing earlier? Her mind grappled for an answer.

He must have sensed her inattention for he prompted helpfully, 'Not all the children had the same diagnosis.'

'Of course!' she muttered, still scrambling to recover the threads of the conversation. 'Actually, four had acute lymphocytic or lymphoblastic leukaemia, the type they call ALL, and the other had one loosely tied to it—non-Hodgkin's lymphoma. These are cancers where the possibility of a viral trigger is very strong, because the peak age for contracting them is between two and six, the age where children first come into a lot of contact with other children at playgroup, kindergarten or school. As in most cases of childhood leukaemia, something goes wrong with the production of lymphocytes.'

She looked up from her study of the coffee and added, 'But you'd know all this.'

He half smiled his agreement. 'Tell me again,' he suggested. 'It's a long time since I actually studied it.'

Was he really interested? Caitlin was wary of assuming too much. The man's moods swung like a pendulum.

'Within both ALL and non-Hodgkins there are subgroups depending on the type of cell affected—B-cell, T-cell, etc. Because of similar cell involvement it's often hard to differentiate between non-Hodgkin's and ALL. In children, the malignant cells tend to grow in a diffuse pattern, not in the lumps and clumps we usually associate with lymphoma.'

'So what you're saying is, the five are more closely related than I'd thought. If that's the case, why did one child die?'

He'd looked at her while he'd been speaking, but before she could reply he swung his head away, gazing out over the railing to where the moon had now risen above the trees and was casting its silvery light across the little park, softening its drabness.

'Perhaps resistance to the treatment—or even a late diagnosis,' Caitlin said, then added quickly before he could take offence, 'The symptoms are so vague—pallor, loss of appetite, a general lassitude. Parents will often take a child to the GP two or three times before a blood test is ordered.'

His head turned towards her and he nodded slowly, then she saw a small, tight smile stretch his lips.

'Not in this town—not now! I take blood if there's even a suspicion it might be leukaemia.'

'Yet you're against me doing some research here that might help alleviate the curse of it for ever.'

Connor sighed, then stood up again, as if his body couldn't contain his emotion when it was seated.

'I'm not against your work but sceptical of what good it can do. The thought of stirring up old enmities again if there's no chance of some end result…'

'Need old enmities be stirred?' she demanded. 'I'm not here testing water or chemicals, I'm here to talk to families. If there's some kind of genetic link—'

'If!' he snorted, disbelief so evident Caitlin wondered if the subject was worth pursuing. 'And if you do, by some miracle, happen to find a link, what can you do?'

'Nothing at the moment,' she admitted, 'but that's no reason not to keep trying. Let's simplify this to a hypothetical. Say, for instance, after DNA testing of the families involved, we find a strand of chromosomal material with five bumps on one side, then find that all the children who contracted cancer had only four bumps, while the children from the same bloodlines but with five bumps didn't—'

'Bumps? Now, there's a precise scientific term!' he muttered, but he'd come closer and seemed interested. 'OK, let's stick with bumps. Are you saying you could add another bump?'

'Not right now, but immunologists are already working on ways of transporting killer T-cells, the cancer-fighting lymphocytes, into humans with cancer, and geneticists are working on infecting bacteria which can enter genetic material and actually alter it. It's being done in test tubes, so eventually it can be done in human patients and at least we'd know what to work on, wouldn't we?'

'A bump-producing germ that could virtually inoculate at-risk children?' he said quietly. 'Put like that, I suppose I can't object to your presence. What do you need from me?'

Connor asked the question but his heart quailed within him as he gave tacit agreement to this woman's presence in Turalla. No matter how discreetly she went about her business, the reason for her visit would soon be known all over town. Was he wrong in anticipating trouble? Raising ghosts with his sense of apprehension?

'Do you know the children? Their families? Anything about their history? What I'd like to do is work out some kind of genealogical chart and see if anything connects.'

Caitlin sounded so earnest he forgot the ghosts and smiled.

'Setting up a theory in order to shoot it down?' he teased, and won a smile that did peculiar things to his internal organs.

'Exactly! It could well be a wild-goose chase, you know, but having this cluster is a unique opportunity to test this particular theory. Look, you've got to start from the fact that the usual incidence of ALL is thirty-three children in every million. What if we ignored the high incidence here in Turalla, and an opportunity to learn something new was lost?'

He glanced down at her hands, clasped around the coffee-mug, and noticed her whitened knuckles. Could she really care so much?

'Is learning something new so important to you?' he asked. 'The be-all and end-all of your life?'

She shrugged but it was a half-hearted attempt at nonchalance.

'Yes, it's important to me,' she stated flatly. 'Whether it's the be-all and end-all I don't know.'

He dropped into his chair so he could see her face.

'Then it's never been tested, has it?' he said. 'You've never had to choose between your chosen path and someone else's?'

He heard his own lingering bitterness in the words and was surprised, thinking it had burnt out long ago. She'd heard it too, for her eyes held questions he certainly wasn't going to answer, but all she said was, 'No. Perhaps I've been fortunate.'

Her voice was dismissive, as if the subject wasn't important, but he couldn't let go of it, couldn't help needling this super-composed woman fate had seen fit to send him.

'And if it ends up just a target, your theory, how do you handle that?'

Caitlin chuckled and he knew she'd fielded that question more than once.

'I set up another, and another and another,' she told him. 'Who knows which one will prove correct, which strand of thought might lead even a small way towards the centre of the puzzle? But we were talking about the children, the families…'

'Lucy Cummings, Harry Jackson, Aaron Wilson and Annabel Laurence.' If he added the child who died, Jonah Neil, it would make two girls and three boys, right on the button statistically as incidence was slightly higher in boys than girls.

But he didn't mention Jonah.

'Naturally, as I'm the only doctor in town they're all my patients, but I rarely see them. I take blood when they're due to go down to the city for follow-up appointments, three-monthly at first, then six-monthly. I think all of them are on yearly visits now. In fact, I seem to remember someone saying Harry doesn't have to go back for two years.'

Simple background information, nothing even vaguely medical, yet the uneasiness returned. Stronger than uneasiness because it had his subconscious considering a holiday—or perhaps a transfer to a hospital a few thousand miles away.

Connor knew he wouldn't leave Turalla when trouble in this beautiful package was standing on its doorstep, hand raised ready to knock—but it didn't stop him wishing!

'I'm sorry, I was miles away,' he said, when her voice recalled him from his wayward thoughts.

'Or wishing you were,' she suggested, a half-smile tilting one side of her mouth upward and pressing a dimple into her cheek. 'I was saying I've already spoken to Lucy's parents about this. I met them when they were down for her check-up last week. I didn't go into details, just said I'd like to look at family backgrounds.'

'And how did they react?' he asked, surprised he hadn't heard anything of this. The rumour mill was usually super-efficient. Perhaps the Cummings family had stayed on for a holiday in the city.

The half-smile became a whole one—neat, even teeth gleaming in the moonlight.

'A bit like you,' she admitted. 'They'd love to have answers to the ''why'' question all parents ask, but they're dubious that anything could be found in past histories. Like most people, they feel if it's genetic their other children would be at risk and they don't want to even consider that thought.'

Surprise, surprise! Connor rubbed his hands through his hair, kneading at his scalp in an effort to find the words he needed. Perhaps he could still dissuade her.

'Added to which, anything genetic, to a parent, seems to imply parental blame,' he said. 'Have you considered the ructions that could cause? Husbands and wives sniping at each other because he or she carried a defective gene? Or taking it further, what about the implications to young people in love—will their marriage plans be thwarted by one of your errant genes?'

She nodded her agreement, but had an answer all ready for him.

'There's a town in the United States where a similar study was done on the incidence of Huntington's chorea. Over there a social worker was available to counsel people who felt at all apprehensive or distressed. Your local counsellor has already been contacted and has agreed to work with me on this, and provide counselling if needed. And genetic counselling is becoming a more accepted part of people's plans for the future. If some link is discovered, isn't it better for a couple to be aware a danger could exist and have their children tested regularly? Children with some forms of leukaemia now have an eighty to ninety per cent chance of being completely cured—testing of children considered at risk could make those statistics even better.'

'OK, I'll grant you that round—although while genetic counselling might be discussed in some places, it's hardly an everyday topic here in Turalla,' he said, hating the fact that the medical Connor was swaying towards her arguments while the emotional man who shared the doctor's skin still felt an inexplicable sense of dread about the whole idea. 'But is there no other way than through the families?'

He didn't say 'all the families' although the dread was

finding focus in the child he hadn't mentioned and the strange, religious, upright man who'd fathered him.

Ezra Neil, husband of the silent Mrs Neil.

The reason the silent Mrs Neil was so silent?

Connor didn't know, but Mrs Neil's behaviour suggested there was a problem somewhere in her life, and Connor couldn't help linking it to Ezra rather than the loss of her son.

'Does it have to be so personal?' he persisted, the wedge of fear again prodding at his rib cage.

She looked into his eyes and he saw a plea in hers—and noticed how her knuckles had whitened again as she gripped the coffee-mug. Did it mean so much to her? Was her job, her livelihood, dependent on it? Why was she so determined? He watched her formulate her reply while his mind pondered those unspoken questions.

'I know there could be problems, but genetic heritage is the obvious place to start because through DNA studies we can link chromosomal similarities to blood lines,' she said quietly. 'I do understand the human side of it, Connor, but is that excuse enough to ignore an opportunity of making a breakthrough in something that is the most common life-threatening disorder of childhood?'

Connor acknowledged her words with upraised hands of surrender and tried not to think about how his name had sounded—kind of husky—on her lips.

'That was a low blow, Caitlin O'Shea, and you know it. I thought scientists shunned emotive arguments.'

She relaxed enough to smile and pushed the coffee-mug away as if she no longer needed its dubious support.

'This scientist might be different,' she said lightly.

Her gaze snagged his and held, and a spark in the depth of those dark, dark eyes suggested she was flirting with him.

He ignored a purely physical response he hadn't felt for quite some time and refused the challenge, saying lightly, 'Outwardly perhaps. You hardly meet the absent-minded,

horn-rimmed-glasses image of a scientific nerd—but I'm
not fooled by the front, Dr O'Shea. I'll reserve my judgement. And I'll be watching every move you make and
whenever possible monitoring your consultations with the
families. If this situation even hints at volatility, I'll pull
the plug on it and let my conscience cope with the con-
sequences.'

She seemed startled and he wondered if her looks were
usually enough to ensure she got exactly what she wanted.

'Hardball, huh?' she said, a smile lighting up her face
once again.

'Very hard,' he assured her, rising to his feet as she
stood up so they were eye to eye across the table.

'Now, shall I walk you home? I took your car over
earlier.' He fished in his pocket and produced her keys,
glancing at his watch as he handed them to her. 'Hell, it's
after ten. I'm sorry I kept you here so late when you've
got gear to unpack. Would you prefer to spend the night
in my spare bedroom and get yourself settled in the morning?'

Caitlin replayed the words in her mind and realised
there was no warmth in the casual invitation. The man
had decided she was trouble and he wanted her to overnight in his house about as much as he wanted her staying
on in this town.

'I'll go across to my new home,' she told him. 'But
you don't have to come. Just point the way.'

He walked back into the kitchen and she followed him,
blinking in the brightness after the soft light on the veranda.

'I'll walk you home,' he repeated. 'I go over about this
time each evening to do a ward round so I'll show you
through the hospital if you like and scrounge you some
supplies from the kitchen so you don't starve to death on
your first morning in town.'

She found herself grinning at his words and, as he bent
down and hefted her bag on to his shoulder, she said,

'Mightn't that be a good thing? It would rid you of your problem.'

He swung around and caught her smile, answering it with a one hundred watt effort of his own.

'It's a point, but think how bad it would look for the staff,' he protested. 'Visiting doctor wastes away on hospital doorstep! The town would never live it down.'

'Give the locals something else to talk about,' she replied, following him down the steps. 'It might even divert them enough for the divisions you talk of to heal over.'

She spoke lightly, joking with him, more relaxed than she'd been all evening, so when he stopped and spun to face her, she was startled. His eyes, dark shadows in his face, seemed to peer into her soul, and the words, when he uttered them, were as bleak and hard as bullets—as cold as death itself.

'The last death didn't heal them.'

CHAPTER THREE

So MUCH for relaxed! The words cast darker shadows than the moon, only these were in Caitlin's heart. No matter how carefully one trod, research, once translated from laboratory to the 'real' world, intruded into people's lives. It was a dilemma all scientists agonised over with depressing regularity.

She loitered by the swings, longing to sit on one of them, to push off with her legs and feel the rush of wind against her skin as she recaptured the careless abandonment of childhood, that total involvement in the physical delight of soaring through the air, all mental turbulence forgotten—if indeed it had ever been known.

'I still do some of my best thinking on those swings. Very late at night when I'm reasonably certain no one will see the local doctor indulging in such a childish pursuit.'

Caitlin stared at him. This was the second time he'd locked unerringly onto her thoughts. Did he read minds, this Connor Clarke, or was the pristine country air transmitting her thoughts as sound waves?

'Do you need a swing often?' she asked, picking up her pace so she moved ahead of him.

'Often enough,' he replied, the tone of his voice slowing her steps. She waited until he came abreast of her so she could see his face to try to judge his mood. 'Out here the roads are long and straight—open invitations for young daredevils to try the thrill of speed—and for all the perception of innocence, a small town is little more than a microcosm of the city. We have lonely people who no longer want to live, marriages where abuse occurs, children who suffer neglect of one kind or another.'

He spoke quietly, looking down into her eyes, then he reached out and tucked a loose strand of hair behind her ear in a curiously gentle gesture.

'Not in epidemic proportions, of course, but such problems in a community that prides itself on knowing what's what almost before it happens can become magnified in importance.' He shrugged and turned away, once again leading her towards the lights of the hospital. 'For both the patients and the doctor, I guess.'

The final sentence drifted back to her and she knew it had been said for her benefit. There was something in the words she should consider, should try to understand. But tiredness had returned in an all-enveloping wave and she was pleased when he swung to the left, obviously forgetting his offer to show her around and bypassing the front door of the hospital. Instead, he guided her towards the rear of the building.

Her car was parked under an awning attached to one side of the small timber dwelling. Two tall eucalypts prevented the moonlight touching the exterior, so the house crouched like a dark animal seeking the protection of the shadows. From fear, or ready to spring?

It was tiredness prompting the fancies, Caitlin knew that, but it didn't stop a shiver rippling down her spine, or a sense of relief when a flash of brightness dispelled the gloom.

'Sensor lights. All the hospital outbuildings have them. We don't run to night patrols or any other security, but Mike Nelson had these installed when he took over as DON. It's a safety precaution as much as anything else. Staff moving from one building to another for any reason could trip and fall in the dark.'

'Or tread on a snake!' Caitlin muttered, as memories of her childhood, dashing from one building to the next in the dark, re-awoke her most primal fear.

'Don't fancy snakes?' Connor teased, opening the front door of the cottage and flicking on an interior light.

'Not even in picture books,' she told him. 'Oh, I know all the theories about them being more scared of humans than we are of them, but I've never seen a snake leap four feet into the air and stand trembling on a table, and until I do I'll go on being the scaredest!'

She peered cautiously around the room, just the thought of the creatures setting her nerves on edge.

Connor noticed the tension in her neck and jaw. Fancy this beautiful and so very together woman admitting to such a fear.

'I wouldn't worry about the house,' he said, hoping to reassure her. 'The way Mrs Neil cleans and vacuums there wouldn't be an ant remaining in residence, let alone a snake. And if you check the windows you'll see they're all screened and the doors, both front and back, fit tightly. That's been done for the air-conditioning so, unless you leave a door open, you should be safe.'

She shrugged as if to ease the tension, and swung to face him, a tired smile playing about her lips.

Such lovely lips—eminently kissable...

Now, where had that thought sprung from? Better stick to snakes, old son. Practical, controllable stuff!

'And if you need further assurance,' he continued, although thoughts of lips—and lack of control—still occupied his mind, 'we've a collection of four part-feral cats living under the veranda at the hospital. The cook feeds them to keep them away from the birds and small mammals but they keep the place free of mice and would soon warn off any snake or lizard foolish enough to venture into their territory.'

This time the smile was real and he read relief as well as humour in it.

'Thanks!' she said. 'I'd actually forgotten all those night fears of snakes I used to have until the lights came on and I automatically looked for one. It's a silly phobia, and maybe by now I've outgrown it, but I'd just as soon not put it to the test tonight.' The smile reached her eyes which gleamed into his as she added, 'Or any night, for that matter.'

Caitlin reached out to take the bag he was lifting off his shoulder.

'Thank you for feeding me, and being so kind in spite of your misgivings about my presence in the town. I've some basic provisions in the car so don't bother about supplies from the kitchen. I'll unpack a few things from the boot and head for bed. In spite of the sleep this afternoon, it's been a long day.'

It was an unmistakable dismissal yet Connor passed her the bag reluctantly. He could offer her a guided tour of the house, but as she could see the kitchen from where they stood, a small U-shaped space divided from this room by a breakfast bar, and the bathroom and bedroom doors were also visible, it might seem foolish. If he hadn't already returned her car keys he could offer to unload the car...

Caitlin could feel his indecision. She could only assume it was because he had more to say on the subject of her research. Did he resent her intrusion so strongly? Had he meant it when he'd said he wanted to monitor her consultations? Was he going to fight her project every inch of the way?

She sighed, not wanting to be at odds with anyone— particularly not this man.

'Haven't you a hospital to visit?' she reminded him, dropping the bag onto a sturdy armchair and propping her body against the back of it. 'It will take me a couple of hours in the morning to set up my files and computer. Perhaps if you've some spare time tomorrow, I could explain how I've planned to do the research and you can point out what might or might not work.'

Her eyes studied his face, watching for any reaction, however slight, but all he did was dip his head as if in agreement, then he raised it and those mesmerising eyes looked into hers.

'Leaving town could be the answer, but I guess that isn't part of your plan. What if I drop in after my early ward round? You up and about by seven?'

He's trying to rile you, she reminded herself, reining in the spark of anger his 'leaving town' remark had caused. Yet only moments ago he'd been kind, reassuring her about the snakes. Maybe if she wasn't so tired she could fathom his mood swings.

Maybe she wouldn't bother!

'Seven's fine by me!' she answered sweetly, and added an equally saccharine smile. Tomorrow would be soon enough to consider Connor Clarke's behaviour. Soon enough for everything!

He left abruptly and the house seemed empty for his going, but surely that was another manifestation of her tiredness. Forcing her attention to practical matters, she unpacked the car, first liberating her PC and setting it up on a table in the bedroom, then stacking all but what she'd need for the night in the living room of the small house. This done, she fell into bed, exhaustion finally grabbing her and dragging her down into a deep, deep sleep. Deep as a mine shaft...

She dreamt of snakes and death, represented not by the old man with a scythe but a kangaroo wearing a wrist-watch. Yet she knew it was Death and the cold fear of the dream lingered when she woke to the lilting melody of the butcher birds' morning chorus and weak, leaf-dappled sunlight beyond the window.

Her travelling alarm showed five-thirty. Hardly her usual wake-up time! If she leapt out of bed right now she could have everything in place before her colleague arrived.

Was 'colleague' the right word? Didn't colleagues work together, not against each other? Would Connor work against her or simply not co-operate? And why was that thought so depressing?

Because he's the first man you've looked at as a man in a long time, her honest self replied. As a man! Emotional, not scientific thinking.

Stick to science.

Lucy Cummings, Harry Jackson, Aaron Wilson and Annabel Laurence. She ran the names through her head like a litany to blot out thoughts of the man who might or might not be a colleague.

And the child who died? She pictured the coloured folder and tried to recall his name.

An incomplete file—thinner than the others—information missing, or never gathered? A biblical name—Isaiah? Jeremiah?

A loud knocking on the door, a voice calling her name. She sat up with a start, glancing automatically at the clock. Seven!

'Come in!' she called, the name Jonah popping into her head at the same time. 'I woke early then must have drifted back to sleep. I'll be out in a minute.'

She pulled on the shirt she'd worn the previous evening and dashed across the hall to the bathroom, not looking towards the front room where her visitor must be waiting. Cold water helped clear her head. She splashed her face, cleaned her teeth, dragged a brush through her hair then reversed her route across the narrow passage, catching a mouth-watering waft of bacon in the air.

Must be the hospital breakfast. Reaching for her jeans, she tugged them on and checked the clock again. Four minutes, not bad.

'I'm sorry to keep you waiting,' she said, then stopped and stared at the scene of domesticity. Connor was in the kitchen, calmly pouring boiling water into coffee-mugs, the breakfast bar set with knives and forks, and centred in front of them a platter containing heaped bacon, eggs, sausages, hash browns, beans and toast. 'You don't have to keep feeding me,' she protested, while her stomach clenched in anticipatory delight and her legs propelled her towards the food.

'It was no trouble—this is only a small portion of the food spread out in the kitchen, waiting to be eaten by patients, staff and possibly wandering minstrels as well. Nellie, our cook, believes in being prepared. I didn't know what you liked apart from cereal so I brought a bit of everything she had on offer,' he explained, waving a hand towards the platter. 'Help yourself.'

'Haven't dieticians put a stop to this kind of breakfast in your hospital?' Caitlin asked, battling her tantalised tastebuds as she chose a strip of bacon, an egg and two slices of toast. 'I thought the nutrition police had banned this culinary bliss years ago.'

He set a mug of coffee in front of her, pulled out a stool and settled down beside her.

'Not in Turalla,' he said cheerfully. 'Although Nellie has swung away from lard and butter. She now uses olive oil and assures me it's doing me good. Actually, we've a number of elderly townspeople who've no family to care for them. One wing of the building has been divided into single rooms so they can use it as a hostel, taking their meals here but free to come and go as they like. They still like their traditional breakfasts and if I say anything against them, Nellie argues that the old folk have survived on this type of food for ninety years, so why change things now?'

Caitlin heard the words but while her mind absorbed them as casual conversation, it was too busy puzzling over her body's reaction to the man's presence on a neighbouring stool to take much interest. Genuine physical symptoms like an unsteadiness behind her ribs—atrial fibrillation?—and a peculiar hesitancy in her breathing. Could she become an asthmatic at twenty-seven?

'Not hungry after all?' he asked.

She glanced towards him and caught amusement in his

eyes. A teasing gleam that stopped her lungs completely and sent her heart into tachycardia.

'I— Yes…' She struggled to find the words she needed, to string one or two together to form some sensible reply.

Impossible with him so close!

Well, that was fixable. She pushed her plate across the bench, then stood up and shifted her stool to the other side.

'Easier to talk if we can see each other,' she said, although the excuse sounded incredibly feeble in her own ears, and she wasn't certain she was up to talking just yet.

Connor watched as she picked up her knife and fork and tackled her breakfast with a determined frown. She was just as lovely in the bright light of morning, possibly more so as her slightly tousled hair provoked unwanted images of her in bed, and the pink flush on her cheeks aroused libidinous and very censurable thoughts.

Was there a special man in her life? Surely so. Another scientist perhaps, as she'd said she'd never had to choose between a person and her career path.

'I'd like to start with one family and work from them,' she said, glancing up at him with her drown-in brown eyes. 'Do you know if one has more connections in the town than the others?'

He hesitated, then silently admitted that, much as he wished she hadn't come, he also didn't want her leaving until he'd had a chance to get to know her a little better— to see if the person inside would match the glorious outer shell. Ignoring all his reservations, he opted for co-operation.

'Aaron Wilson's mother is a Russell, so if you're looking at family links you won't do better than starting with the Russells,' he suggested. 'They run the bakery in town and old Granny Russell is considered the main trunk of the local grapevine.'

'Will she talk to me? Co-operate? I wouldn't like to get offside with anyone at this early stage.'

Caitlin's eyes held his, her commitment plain to read, but something else in the lustrous darkness puzzled him. A plea, perhaps.

For his support?

Well, he was giving that.

His blessing?

No, he couldn't go that far. His desire to know her better hadn't entirely blotted out the nameless anxiety the fax had caused.

'I'm sure Granny will talk to you. She knows the history of the town, and in these parts predates the telephone, radio and television for the dissemination of news. She's usually more accurate as well.'

'Then I'll start with her,' Caitlin agreed, smiling cheerfully as she turned back to her breakfast. 'Were you serious about sitting in on consultations? Will I have to make a time to see her that suits you as well?'

She glanced up again, challenging him this time.

'Talking to Granny will help you with background information,' he conceded. 'I guess you can do that on your own.'

'Just keep clear of your patients?' she teased, and Connor's anxiety curdled into fear again.

He pushed aside his breakfast, trying to confront this bogey—to analyse it, pin it down. He wasn't a man prey to presentiments or fancies, so why this nagging sense of dread?

The clear, slightly sun-brushed skin of her forehead wrinkled into a frown and he sighed, shook his head and finally replied.

'All the townsfolk are my patients. But as far as your work is concerned, I'll ask the parents if they're willing to talk to you. It will be up to them to decide what they want to do, and also for them to decide if they'd like me to be present.'

Caitlin was glad she'd shifted. His pompous-doctor

tone of voice made her want to belt him one! And to think her body had been attracted to him!

'Don't make it sound as if they'll be facing the guillotine,' she snapped, using words instead of her fist. 'I'm looking for genetic links, not prying into their personal affairs. Genealogy is an increasingly popular hobby these days. For all you know, someone in town may already be working on a family tree that will help me trace the bloodlines of the children involved. It's no big deal, Connor, so why the drama?'

He seemed startled by her anger, as if her words had woken him from some private reverie, for he frowned and studied her face, his eyes both sombre and watchful.

'No drama!' he said lightly, lifting broad shoulders in a seemingly casual shrug. About as casual as microsurgery, judging by the tightness of the tendons in his neck, the stiffness in his muscles only partially concealed by another pale blue shirt. 'I'll get my receptionist to drop by to introduce you to Granny. She's in hospital at the moment, and bored to death, so will welcome a visit. My receptionist's name is Melissa and she's a local, so anything else you want to know about the town, ask her.'

He's distancing himself from the project, Caitlin guessed, but this was hardly the moment to confront him with it. No, he'd made his opposition plain from the beginning and, no matter how attractive her body found him, it was better this way.

She stood up.

'Thanks for that, and for breakfast.' She nodded to her pile of possessions just inside the front door. 'Now I'd better get on with unpacking.'

Would he take the hint and go? Given his reluctance to be involved, she'd thought he would, but, no, the contrary man seemed stuck on the stool, although he swung around to watch her progress.

'Can I lift something for you? Computer? Or are you working on a laptop?'

'I've both,' she replied with a bluntness just short of rudeness. Why didn't he go? Why was he remaining with such rock-like persistence, taking up space in the small house, breathing her air and making her skin feel prickly? 'And I can carry a PC. In fact, it's all set up and ready to go.'

He glanced around the room and raised an eyebrow.

'There's a table in the bedroom, I'm using that.'

'I could shift the table out here for you if that would be more convenient,' he offered.

He obviously had no intention of leaving!

'Thanks, but I like it where it is. I'm used to working that way.' She heard the defensiveness in her voice, guessed at his reaction, but before she could think of some diversionary tactic he'd pounced.

'Ideal bedroom companion, a computer. Obedient, quiet, undemanding.'

His eyes were smiling at her. Lips too, but she was trying not to think about his lips. She responded, relaxing slightly but retaining a wariness in case this mood change was a trap.

'And never answers back,' she added. 'Actually, I do a lot of my theoretical work at home, often at night. It's convenient to be able to fall straight from the chair into bed.'

Caitlin felt warmth tingling in her cheeks and was sorry she'd mentioned beds. Not that he seemed to notice. He was staring at her and shaking his head as if totally bemused.

'And that's your life? Work until you drop, fall into bed then get up and work again?'

'I didn't say that,' she retorted, although the bleak sentence just about summed up her life of late. 'It's not like that all the time.'

Connor's smile broadened. 'Methinks the lady, et cetera,' he said, then he glanced at his watch, eased himself off the stool and began to gather up the dirty plates.

'I'll do that,' she said quickly, wanting him out of the place as soon as possible. His mood swings were easier to handle than his smiles.

'OK, then I'll be off to work. Mike's extension is four, mine is seven, if you want to talk to either of us. Melissa gets in at about nine. I do an outpatients clinic at the hospital this morning so she'll be free. I'll ask her to come over as soon as she's dealt with the mail.'

He walked past her and was out the door so swiftly she was left staring blankly after him.

Melissa arrived at ten, a buxom brunette with a bright smile and a warm welcoming manner.

'Connor said you're here to do research,' she said, after introducing herself and dropping a bright pink plastic folder on the breakfast bar. 'About the leukaemia. I was working for Dr Robinson when the other people came. Boy, was there trouble in the town!'

Her eyes shone with remembered excitement.

'It didn't bother you?' Caitlin asked, contrasting this reaction to Connor's grim warnings.

'Nah! It brought the place to life for a while! Gave everyone something to talk about. Probably got a lot of old grievances sorted out—personal tiffs that people could settle, pretending it was to do with the scientific stuff. Everything was jumping but no one got hurt. Even the shots were fired after most people were in bed and it was probably kids who'd had a few drinks.'

Caitlin smiled at her enthusiasm, then shook her head.

'I'm afraid I'm not here to stir up that kind of excitement,' she said. 'I'm looking into family histories, but what you've told me might make things easier. Do many people feel the way you do about "the war" as Connor called it? See it more as a "letting off steam" occasion than an actual rift between different members of the community?'

Melissa's smile faded and she frowned for a moment,

then brightened up, her thoughts almost readable on her expressive features.

'I think most folk saw it my way. Bit of a lark, really.' She hesitated, the frown once again knitting her brows. 'Except for Dr Robinson disappearing like that. We all stopped laughing then. The whole town was involved in the search, one way or another, and that ended all the silly squabbling and name-calling. We've always been a town that pulls together when there's trouble and the doctor disappearing so unexpectedly—well, it brought us all together again.'

Connor had told it differently but, then Connor wasn't a local. Neither was he a gossip—well, he clammed up whenever his predecessor was mentioned. Making Caitlin more curious rather than less.

'Did you know you had to search for her?' she asked Melissa. 'Was there some reason why you knew she was lost—that she hadn't just got into her car and left town of her own accord?'

'It was the car,' Melissa explained. 'Mr Neil found it parked out in the State Forest not far from his place. It wasn't locked and she'd left the keys and a bottle of mineral water in it as if she wasn't going to be away long. Mr Neil drove in and told the sergeant.'

She shivered theatrically, prompting Caitlin to ask, 'Is it a scary place, the State Forest?'

Melissa chuckled. 'Not the place, the man—Ezra Neil.' She gave another shudder. 'My Mum says Ezra's an Old Testament name, and that's exactly what he looks like— a biblical prophet who preached about hell and damnation, and all that eye-for-an-eye stuff. I mean, fancy naming your son Jonah, when everyone knows a Jonah is someone who brings bad luck. Poor kid, he never had a chance. He's the one who died, you know. Of leukaemia.'

'Not because of his name,' Caitlin pointed out quietly, the mention of the child's death reminding her she was here to work, not gossip. And why the work was so important, whatever the townspeople might think of her intrusion into their lives. A sense of urgency swept over her.

She picked up the file Melissa had prepared and opened it. Melissa stepped closer.

'I haven't put in the patient files because Connor said to get permission from the families before giving you them, but I'll phone them all this morning and drop the files in later.'

She pointed to a list on the first page.

'When Connor told me you wanted to know about relationships, I jotted down some notes. I know Granny Russell is related to Anne Jackson, although I'm not sure how, and the Cummingses are an old farming family so they could be linked up somewhere. Annabel Laurence's dad is the mine manager, but her mother was a Snape and they've been here since the gold-rush days when a Snape ran a saloon on the goldfields. Mrs Laurence doesn't like people talking about that because she's a bit grand now she's married.'

Caitlin smiled.

'Thanks, Melissa,' she said. 'These notes are exactly what I need to get me started. Connor said Granny— should I call her that or Mrs Russell?—was in hospital at the moment and I could see her there.'

'Call her Granny—everyone does. Even Connor, who was ever so stiff and formal with the patients when he first arrived. I'll take you over to see her now if you like.'

Caitlin felt the first stirrings of excitement as she grabbed a notebook and followed Melissa across to the hospital. It was always like this at the beginning of a project—the thrill of the chase. Seeking clues and information and fitting them together, trying the facts this way and that, searching for a pattern—or a break in a pattern— that would lead to the next stage of a new discovery.

Connor Clarke could scoff at her lifestyle, but surely this excitement was as great as any other—greater than the few sexual adventures she'd undertaken, that was for sure. Although why she was thinking of Connor and sexual adventures in the same breath she didn't know.

Or could pretend she didn't!

Melissa led the way through a side door and along a corridor past empty rooms, finally pausing outside one that was obviously occupied—the noise from the television providing the clue.

'Granny, this is Dr Caitlin O'Shea,' Melissa said, after greeting the elderly woman on the bed and answering a number of questions about the health of her family.

'The girl who's come to do research?' Granny said, turning towards Caitlin, bright, bird-like eyes alive with interest and intelligence. 'Anthea Cummings told Alan, that's my granddaughter's husband, young Aaron's father. Bet that Connor told you to start with me because I'm a gossip, didn't he? Well, I don't tell harm of anyone, but anything else you want to know about who's who in this town, I reckon I can help you out.'

The flow of words stopped abruptly, leaving Caitlin fumbling for something to say.

'Th-thank you,' she stuttered, then Melissa came to her rescue.

'Why don't you sit down?' she suggested to Caitlin. 'I've got to get back to work.'

'Are you sure you're up to talking now?' Caitlin asked Granny Russell before taking the chair Melissa indicated.

The old lady laughed.

'At my age, if you put something off till later, later mightn't find you home—if you get my drift.'

It was an innocent enough remark but for some reason Caitlin thought of Connor's predecessor—the woman who'd died such a lonely, terrible death—and though she drew the chair up close to Granny's bed and settled into it, a nameless fear hovered around her like a cold, damp mist.

CHAPTER FOUR

CAITLIN spent three hours with the elderly woman. Granny talked about her grandparents, who had been among the first white children in the district, born in primitive conditions to women who had followed their men out into 'the bush'.

Their families had been large, medical support scanty, but in Granny's tales, those women had lived out their lives in rough bark shanties, brought up their surviving children with strength and courage and shared an abiding optimism in the new country's future.

Granny had delighted in regaling her guest with the medical horrors of those days—childbed fever, stillborn infants and rough bush do-it-yourself medicine, but she had drawn links between those pioneering families and given Caitlin other names.

'You've been a wonderful help,' Caitlin said, when she sensed Granny was tiring. 'I'd like to come back and see you again, not to ask questions but to listen to your stories.'

Granny smiled at her.

'I'd like that,' she said, and reached out to take Caitlin's hand. 'Did Connor tell you what was wrong with me?'

Caitlin shook her head.

'Although I did a full medical degree and worked in hospitals for a few years, I'm here as a researcher, not a doctor,' she explained. 'He wouldn't talk to me about his patients.'

'Phooey!' Granny snorted. 'He's far too uptight about things like that—as if everyone in town doesn't know who's got what disease.'

She smiled at Caitlin, then added, 'I've got it too, leukaemia, but a different kind to what the children had. They could treat it with that chemo stuff but it'd make me so sick, what's the point? So Connor brings me in when I get tired and puts good blood back into me and that keeps me going a bit longer. We've talked about it, Connor and I, how it will be. He's a good man.'

This recommendation stayed with Caitlin as she walked up to the town to get some basic supplies. She'd drive to the supermarket later to shop properly, but after the session with Granny she'd needed to stretch her legs and breathe some fresh air.

Needed to get the 'good man' out of the forefront of her mind, too.

She reached the bakery to find it packed with customers, so she pulled out her notebook, studying her notes while she waited to be served. *Ask Mrs Jenkins—see James at the garage.* It was as if Granny understood the importance of accuracy and had added these people as corroboratory sources, like annotations in a textbook.

'Help you, miss?'

'Sorry! I'd like a poppy seed bagel and a loaf of sliced wholemeal,' Caitlin said, wondering where all the other customers had gone. Surely she wasn't turning into the much-caricatured absent-minded scientist.

'You're the research person, aren't you?' the plump assistant asked cheerfully as she passed the plastic-wrapped bread to Caitlin and grasped a pair of stainless-steel tongs to delve into the cabinet for the bagel. 'I'm related to Aaron through the Russells. Not real close, mind you, but I'm one of the red ones.'

She flung back a mane of extravagantly curled red hair.

'Any red hair you see in this town, there's sure to be some Russell in them somewhere, although Granny and young Aaron's family are black Russells. Mostly.'

Caitlin watched as her informant manoeuvred the captured bagel into a crisp white paper bag. She knew news travelled fast in country towns, but this fast? And as to opposition, apart from Connor, everyone she'd met so far had greeted her with enthusiasm, not doubts and fore-warnings of disaster. OK, so it was only three people, hardly a widespread sample, but all three had been unan-imous in their interest.

'That's three dollars fifty,' the woman added, plonking the white package on the counter. 'Do you think we'll be on TV again? The town, I mean?'

Uh-oh! Was this what lay behind the communal inter-est? The lure of momentary stardom on the small screen? Caitlin counted out some change and handed it to the woman.

'I really doubt it,' she said, but her denial hadn't been heard, for the woman was speaking again, explaining how the front of the shop had been in the first shot and her daughter had been coming out at that very moment. Fleeting moments of glory!

'Great!' Caitlin said heartily, knowing a response of awe or wonder was indicated. 'Well, it's been nice talking to you. I'll see you again.'

She made her escape, her head jostling with thoughts of red Russells and TV cameras. Even if her research proved successful, she knew it would be a beginning, not the kind of headline-grabbing breakthrough TV news de-voured with nightly gusto.

People nodded to her as she walked along the street. Did they all know who she was, or was it their customary politeness to a stranger? She nodded back, and kept walk-ing, past a newsagent, a shoe shop, a narrow-fronted su-permarket and up to the hotel on the corner. Across the road, people walked in and out of the post office, and further down the street she could see a bank and fresh-produce market. Typical country town—a wide main street with dusty vehicles parked at an angle to the kerb.

Yet not so typical if Connor was to be believed. Rounding the corner beneath the overhanging veranda of the old hotel, she pulled the bagel out of the bag. Now she was out of the main street—out of the public eye—she could satisfy the demands of her stomach and eat it on her way home.

Home? Could she call that sparsely furnished temporary dwelling home? She finished the bagel and grinned to herself.

Yep! While she had a bed and her beloved computer, with a modem to link her to the lab, anywhere could be home.

Above her, a bird called to his mate, and she found her grin fading. Had Connor been right to scorn her life? Shouldn't there be more?

She shrugged the questions aside. One day! She'd always told herself that one day she'd want more—perhaps a man, possibly marriage, probably children. But first she had to cement her place in her chosen scientific field, make sure the niche she was carving for herself with such determined dedication, stubbornly butting her head against the brick walls of doubt and prejudice, was secure.

Crossing the road to the hospital, she paused on the pavement, seeing the child she'd once been flying high on the swing. Was she still like that child—always wanting to go higher and higher? Would 'one day' never come because of her ambition?

'Dr O'Shea!'

The male voice drew her back to the real world. Mike Nelson stood on the veranda of the hospital, beckoning her.

She walked briskly towards him, pleased to be diverted from such uncustomary and puzzling thoughts.

'Your boss phoned,' Mike said when she was close enough for normal conversation. 'Said he'd tried to email you some new information on the viral research, but the email bounced back so he sent it to the hospital computer.' Mike handed her a folder with a sheaf of paper in it. 'This is it. On a more personal note, my wife also phoned. Said she'd already asked Connor to eat with us tonight and wondered if you'd like to join us.'

Caitlin felt a familiar irritation flicker down her spine. If there was one thing she hated when she was working, it was social invitations. They forced her into making polite noises and showing interest in other subjects while her mind was grappling with tenuous and unstable theories.

Still, she'd hardly started working and she needed all the co-operation she could garner in this town. She smiled at Mike.

'I'd be delighted. What time and where?'

He returned her smile.

'Seven. I'll ask Connor to drive you, it's silly taking two cars. See you then.'

Mike turned away, disappearing through the front door of the hospital.

Caitlin stared after him, thinking about his smile. If he'd been a woman she'd have suspected it was smug—a little unsubtle matchmaking at work here?

And *that* thought brought its own reaction—the slightly breathless feeling and arrhythmias again.

Ridiculous! she scolded herself, as she made her way around to her temporary home. It was too soon to be imagining an attraction to Connor Clarke, and 'one day' was still a long way off!

Forcing her mind back to work mode, she glanced at the information Mike had given her, sorted her own notes into order and entered some of the data into the computer. Then, using Melissa's lists, she phoned the Laurence and Jackson homes to make appointments for the following day.

Neither Judy Laurence nor Anne Jackson—'it's Ms not Mrs'—seemed surprised by her call. On the contrary, they seemed interested, even eager. Both would be happy to see her on the following day and, no, neither felt Connor's presence would be necessary.

That's one up to me, Dr Clarke, Caitlin thought, surprising herself with her gleeful delight. She jotted down
the appointment times beside the addresses, and wondered
what he'd have to say about it when she saw him later.

Connor came at seven to collect her. Caitlin was ready,
dressed in a conservative calf-length skirt and shirt she'd
brought with her, hoping to impress the country people
with a 'sensible' and 'practical' image. She'd also decided
not to mention work. If he wanted to discuss it, let him
bring it up.

Reminding herself of this, she opened the door to
him—a tall, well-built man wearing fawn chinos and a
dark jade shirt that would no doubt highlight the green in
his eyes. Although he was standing in the glare of the
security light outside her door, she couldn't see his eyes,
for he had turned towards the hospital where someone had
let out a piercing wolf-whistle.

'That's Nellie,' he grumbled, as Caitlin stepped out to
join him and pulled the door shut behind her. 'Can't bear
to think she might be missing something. I should go over
and tell her we're just going up to Mike's for dinner, and
that it's strictly business.'

'Well, heaven forbid she might think it was a date,'
Caitlin muttered scathingly, disconcerted by her reaction
to his words.

He turned towards her and chuckled.

'Sorry! That sounded rude, didn't it? Incidentally, you
should lock the door when you're not here. Not that I
think anyone would steal anything, but there are curious
people everywhere. They'd not see anything wrong in
walking into an unlocked house to check out your possessions.'

'A computer and a bed?' Caitlin teased, pleased his
mood had lightened. 'Anyway, as far as I know, there's
no key. Certainly not one in the lock.'

Connor looked down at her and frowned. So much for a lightened mood!

'There should be a key,' he said gruffly. 'I'll go over and tell Nellie to keep an eye out tonight and find one for you tomorrow.'

He strode away, halted suddenly, then turned back towards her.

'Come along, I'll introduce you.'

Gracious invitation, she thought as she followed his tall figure across to the hospital. What on earth was eating the man?

Connor took the steps in one bound, then turned to see if the visitor was following.

Which was a mistake. He should have continued to ignore her. It would have caused fewer problems in his groin.

'You there, Nellie?' he called, motioning Caitlin into the section of the kitchen accessible to all. 'This is Dr O'Shea. We're both going up to Mike's for dinner and there's no key for her front door. She's got a computer over there and I wouldn't like sticky fingers mucking up her programs so keep an eye on the place, would you?'

He watched the two women shake hands, ignoring his words completely as they exchanged pleasantries. Still, their conversation gave him time to take another look at Caitlin—a long, careful look while he puzzled over why such a prim outfit should increase the wretched woman's sexiness, not detract from it.

'I said go off and enjoy yourselves,' Nellie repeated, waving her hand to shoo them out of the kitchen. 'I'm done here till supper-time so I'll be sitting out the back, blowing a bit of smoke around. No trouble to keep an eye on the house.'

He opened his mouth to remonstrate—again—about Nellie's nicotine addiction, then shut it. Who was he to be giving orders to other people about their lives when his own had been so thoroughly dislocated by this woman's arrival in town?

Caitlin had said goodbye and walked away. He followed, more slowly now, feeling the night air fold around him, smelling a faint sweet perfume as if the beautiful visitor trailed some special scent.

'Your carriage is over this way,' he said, embarrassed by the thought. Now he hurried to catch up. He took her arm and led her towards his hefty Landcruiser. 'It's not as flashy as your speed machine, but it's practical out here.'

She smiled up at him and he felt a peculiar hollowness in his chest, as if his lungs had gone on holiday, and taken his heart with them.

'My dad drove a Landcruiser,' she told him. 'I got my licence in one of these.'

And without waiting for him to open the door, she did the honours herself and swung up into the passenger seat, totally unaware of him as anything other than a chauffeur for the night—thankfully unaware of his reaction to her.

'How did you get on with Granny?' he asked, breaking a silence that seemed too loud.

'Fine. She's great,' Caitlin responded, but her tone was distracted, and when she turned towards him, the anxiety that now accompanied him everywhere like an unwanted shadow returned. 'In fact, so was Melissa, and the woman in the bakery, and even Nellie seemed happy to have me here. So far, Dr Clarke, you're the only one who's made negative noises about my research in the town. Why's that?'

Because I'm the only one with enough sense to see where it could lead?

No, that not only sounded patronising, it was.

And he could hardly use a presentiment of danger, an inexplicable fear, as an excuse.

'Let's wait and see,' he compromised. 'Remember, I'm

also a stranger here. Perhaps I'm reading the situation wrongly—overreacting.'

Yet even as he spoke the placatory words his gut wrenched with memories of Angie—of the white skeletal bones and remnants of hair and flesh he'd had to touch and handle as he'd sought answers on the autopsy table.

It was no good telling himself her death was unrelated to what had been happening in the town at the time she'd disappeared when every instinct denied this assertion. Those same instincts—back when Angie had been missing for a couple of months—had prompted him to apply for the post in Turalla and had convinced him he needed to set his own ambition aside, at least until he'd tried to find out more.

Connor glanced towards his passenger who was looking around with the innocent interest of any visitor, and shook his head.

After two years in Turalla, quietly seeking clues to Angie's disappearance, he'd been almost ready to believe her death had been what everyone said it was—an accident. Now one brief faxed message had short-circuited his brain—one beautiful blonde had thrown the switch and, in his mind at least, fused the past and present.

'Is this a new housing estate? The height's unexpected. Walking uptown the area looks completely flat.'

It took him a moment to work out what Caitlin had said, to regain the equanimity he needed for normal conversation.

'About five years old. The hills begin here with this slight rise, then run parallel to each other out across the plains for about forty miles. You don't realise how orderly they are until you're in the air. From a plane they look like lines drawn on a map. It's some kind of geological phenomenon.'

Normal conversation? He sounded like a schoolteacher.

'This is Mike's place.'

Had she heard the relief in his voice? Probably, for she

was out of the car before he had the engine turned off, and was looking down at the streetlights which marked the straight grids of the town.

Sue welcomed them both, kissing him warmly and shaking hands with Caitlin, chattering on about how nice it was to have a new face at the hospital, even if it was only on a temporary basis.

'Let them come in,' Mike protested, ushering them all through the door. He led Caitlin to a comfortable chair, adding apologetically, 'Sue is always so pleased to have adult conversation, she tends to get over-excited.'

His wife threw a playful jab at his shoulder. 'I've got the qualifications to do your job. How about I take over for a week and let you handle the ankle-biters?'

'I bet he wouldn't last a day,' Connor said, but his eyes were on Caitlin who was smiling at the by-play, a relaxed, natural smile that lit up her eyes and put a glow on her skin.

Or was that make-up? He really didn't know. The only certainty was that he wanted to keep on looking at her—which would be hard if he persuaded her to go away.

'He's lost to us,' Sue said in a mournful voice, and he spun around to see her smirking at him—in fact, Mike was also smirking.

'I'll have a light beer,' he said, hoping that was what they'd asked. The laughter which greeted his reply told him he'd guessed wrong. Even Caitlin was laughing, a low, throaty sound that seemed to ripple in the air before settling in his ears.

'I'll get it,' Mike responded. 'Perhaps you'd better come with me. You can open the wine and I'll ask you again if the new Blair is a girl or boy. I left early this afternoon. Ellie was still in the delivery suite.'

Connor groaned. Talk about foot in mouth!

'She had a boy,' he said, following Mike into the kitchen, but Caitlin's laughter followed him, like an echo he wanted to hear again and again.

Caitlin was glad he'd gone. She'd met attractive men before but none who'd caused this dizzy feeling, as if her body had been spun out of balance.

'What children do you have?' she asked Sue, a petite redhead. A red Russell? she wondered as Sue listed her brood.

'Katrina, Peter, Jessica and Mark. The last two are twins, giving me four under five. Don't ever think having two at once is an easy way of getting your family over and done with. They're double trouble, nothing more.'

She went on to list the twins' latest exploits and iniquities, but Caitlin heard the strong maternal love beneath the gripes in the other woman's voice. Was she missing something, not having children? Would she still have time for a family, once she'd got where she was going?

A loud cry off-stage had Sue out of her chair, and out of the room, in seconds.

Mike and Connor returned, and Caitlin forgot children and the future, intent only on getting through an evening in Connor's presence without revealing the effect he had on her.

'So? Did you have a successful session with Granny?' Mike asked, handing her a glass of wine and lifting his beer in a traditional salute.

'Granny Russell? How does she fit into your research?' Sue returned, demanding answers. 'Unless it's on longevity, or geriatrics with extraordinary memories. I thought you were here about the children who had leukaemia?'

Caitlin smiled at her.

'I am. I'm just looking at it from a different angle—seeking genetic links.'

Sue took the glass of beer Connor offered and sipped at it, frowning thoughtfully.

'Well, finding genetic links in this town shouldn't be too hard. Before the mine was opened, just about everyone was related to each other—which makes it very difficult to gossip about anyone! You could have a field day here.'

'Too many relationships can be as bad as too few,' Caitlin explained. 'It's hard to untie the skeins to see the single threads.'

'Then couldn't you begin with the children who had leukaemia—with their genetic make-up? I was reading an article on DNA mapping in a medical journal recently,' Mike said.

'Surely you have DNA information on the children who contracted the disease?' Connor added, his voice expressing his hope that she might not have to pursue this other course.

Caitlin nodded, taking time to calm the prick of anger. OK, so she'd known she didn't have this man's support, but did he have to be so eager to be rid of her?

Choosing her words with care, she said, 'We have the results of blood tests from the children who were affected but no one at the time did DNA tests on the samples. DNA testing is expensive, so it's not done unless there's a reason.'

'And you're looking for a reason—I can follow that,' Sue said, beaming at Caitlin. 'What will you need?'

Caitlin smiled at her enthusiasm, wishing it was easy to explain.

'I won't really know until I find it but, say, for instance, I discover that all the children had an ancestor in common—'

'How far back?' Sue demanded, and Mike laughed.

'Let the woman finish a sentence,' he suggested.

'That's another thing I don't know,' Caitlin told her. 'We know some recessive or mutated genes can skip generations, but I've a time restriction as well, so I'm thinking perhaps great-great.'

'OK, I've got that.' Sue prompted her to continue but one look at Connor's face suggested he'd had more than enough.

Caitlin hesitated, and Connor, perhaps sensing the reason for her hesitation, said, 'Go on.'

She did, but reluctantly, still feeling his opposition. 'Say all the children had the same ancestor, but as well as the five who contracted the disease there were another forty children with the same blood lines, and maybe twenty of them would have been within the peak age group for developing leukaemia.'

'So you'd DNA-test the ones who didn't get it as well as the ones who did?' Sue said, and Caitlin nodded.

'But first,' she warned, 'I've got to find out if such bloodlines exist. If they don't then that's another theory gone west and I have to start again.'

'Maybe you could DNA-test the whole town,' Sue suggested. 'Get a mighty sample to play with.'

'I think there are ethical constraints there,' Connor reminded her.

'And Caitlin's already mentioned the cost,' Mike added.

'And time!' Sue was now arguing against herself. 'Didn't I read where a DNA test could take up to six weeks?'

Caitlin answered her.

'Yes, but new processes are being developed all the time, including one where quite complicated tests can be done in two days. Instead of the results being printed out in the familiar ''bar code'' result, the make-up of the DNA is shown as letters of the alphabet.'

'And I thought bar codes were for supermarkets,' Sue said, rising to her feet again. 'I want you all to stop this conversation right now while I dish up the dinner, then you can explain to me, Caitlin. It's time my brain had something more challenging than Lego houses and nursery rhymes.'

But the dinner conversation wasn't on genetic testing; instead, it ranged far and wide, only returning to the reason for Caitlin's presence in the town when they were sipping their coffee.

'I know you've both been avoiding the subject,' Sue said, looking first at Connor, then at Caitlin. 'But I'm serious about wanting to know more about DNA and your project, Caitlin. I'm happy at the moment, being at home with the kids, but I do want to go back to nursing eventually and I don't want to be left too far behind. Forgetting the technical stuff for the moment, what are you going to do once you've done your family trees and got your samples?'

'I can look at both similarities and differences in their genetic make-up. I'm actually working from the premise of a viral cause and trying to find out why it affects some people and not others.'

'What genetic structure predisposes one person to be immune while others aren't? Yes, I can see that,' Mike said.

Caitlin smiled at him, pleased by his interest, praying for his support. She had a feeling she'd need plenty of that in the future—particularly with Connor so against her work.

'The benefit of a small town is that—'

'You're likely to have a common pool of breeding stock,' Sue said slowly. 'Fertile ground for a geneticist.'

'Makes us sound like a mob of cattle,' Mike protested. 'I'm glad I'm an outsider.'

'But I'm not,' Sue said.

Caitlin heard constraint in her voice and felt a coolness in the air, as if the easy camaraderie between them had been stirred by a chill wind. She glanced at Connor, who had warned her about this, and read the condemnation in his eyes.

'Being from the town doesn't automatically put your children on a danger list. In fact, there may never be a danger list!' he said to Sue, leaning a little closer to her as if to offer physical comfort. 'As Caitlin said before, she might prove nothing—it's just a theory and so many theories lead to dead ends.'

'But if it did turn into something, I'd certainly want you and the children tested,' Mike said. 'Even if we discovered there was a genetic possibility of one of them contracting ALL. At least then we'd know to keep an eye on him or her—have regular blood tests taken. It would be a safeguard.'

'But the fear…' Sue whispered, the words only a breath above a whisper.

Connor glanced at Caitlin and read the dawning comprehension in her eyes. He should have felt satisfaction, but sympathised instead. Until she spoke—angered, he was certain, by her own moment of doubt.

'So do I not proceed because it's going to dangle the sword of Damocles above some heads?' she demanded. 'Do we deny ourselves the slim possibility of finding a clue to the prevention of one form of cancer because we don't want to upset the town?'

She was asking Connor, not Sue, so he answered.

'Nothing is ever that cut and dried. Starting something like this is like casting a stone into a large pond. Who knows how far the ripples will spread, or what they might wash to the surface?' He reached out and touched her lightly on the hand. 'I know all the logical arguments and agree that Turalla presents a unique opportunity for your work, but I wish we could foresee the problems.'

'And have strategies set in place to deal with them?' Mike smiled as he spoke. 'It's a great theory, mate, but you know as well as I do it's near impossible in practice. Like everything else, we'll have to wait and see—and cope with any fallout if and when it happens. As Caitlin said, she can't not do the work because something *might* happen.'

Connor looked at his friend. Hard to explain that it wasn't 'might' that worried him but a presentiment of danger which he, the most prosaic of men, had never felt before. No, Mike would laugh at him and tell him he must be sickening for something.

He glanced towards Caitlin who was talking quietly to Sue, about children—healthy children.

Perhaps he *was* sickening for something. It would explain a lot of things.

But not why his eyes were drawn to her face, his ears to her voice—his body, if he didn't have it under such iron control, to hers!

'Perhaps you'd better take him home,' Mike suggested, and the two women laughed.

'Was I snoring?' he countered.

'No,' Sue assured him. 'Just not with us. I asked you three times if you'd be golfing on Saturday. It's my turn, remember.' She turned to Caitlin. 'Mike and I take turns to play week and week about—the other minds the kids. Do you play?'

Caitlin shook her head, fielding a slight stab of regret that she'd never learnt—then reminding herself work was more important to her.

'Not that it matters while I'm up here,' she replied. 'I'd prefer to get the research done even if it means working through the weekends.'

'The sooner you finish, the sooner you can be out of the place, is that it?' Connor asked, and Caitlin spun to face him, reacting to a hardness in the question, not the words.

'But you can't work all the time,' Sue told her, before Caitlin could deny Connor's assertion. 'Sunday night's always barbecue night at Connor's. Half the hospital turns up, so that's one date you can't avoid.'

Caitlin waited for Connor's eyes to second the invitation, to show some gleam of hospitality if not enthusiasm for her presence. No go! They were as darkly sombre as they'd been earlier when he'd scolded her for not locking the door. Was there another reason why he didn't want her in Turalla? Perhaps his concern wasn't for the town—perhaps he had some other agenda.

'We should be on our way,' was all he said, and Caitlin took the hint, thanking Mike and Sue, promising Sue she'd keep in touch and, yes, meet her for coffee uptown one day. She followed Connor out the door, and felt the cool night air brush against her skin.

'They're good people,' he said as he opened the car door for her.

'Do you think I can't see that?' she demanded, thinking he was attacking her again, however obliquely.

He touched her arm, a soothing gesture that failed in its effect—instead, sending ripples of alarm along her nerves.

'Hey, I wasn't meaning anything beyond those words. They're nice folk, I like them—that's the beginning and the end.'

She looked up at him. He met her eyes and what she saw there made her forget Mike, and Sue, and research—and how to breathe.

'It's the moonlight,' she muttered to herself, hoisting her body into the car and pulling the door shut before he had a chance to do his polite bit.

'That's all?' he asked when he joined her in the vehicle. She stared at him, then realised he must have heard her words. 'I hope so,' he added obscurely.

She shifted in her seat, made restless by the feeling of confinement in the spacious car. Connor must be taking up too much space, stealing too much air, for his presence to be affecting her like this.

Half smiling at her own nonsensical thoughts, she studied him. Straight, firm profile—slightly jutting chin. A stubborn man? She'd have guessed that even without the chin. She followed the line of his neck, his shoulder, down his arm to the hand resting easily on the steering-wheel. Long fingers, slim and shapely. Would they have a deceptive strength? Be able to hold a woman captive in an iron clasp, yet still caress a breast with a silken touch?

The absurd fancy made her chuckle.

'Is it a joke worth sharing?' he asked.

'Definitely not,' she replied, grateful the shadows hid her burning cheeks.

'Pity!' he murmured. 'A good joke can sometimes ease the tension.'

'I'm not tense with you,' she protested.

And she didn't need his drawled, 'Really?' to underline the lie.

'Well, you haven't been exactly welcoming,' she pointed out.

'No? I thought I'd done the welcome thing quite well.'

She turned suspiciously towards him and caught the gleam of teeth that told her he was teasing, but she wasn't ready to concede just yet.

'Towards me, but not my work,' she argued.

'And is that not possible? Is your work so intertwined with who you are that you daren't stand alone without it?'

The smile was gone and she felt his scorn scorch the words. Yet she felt it was important to answer honestly.

'I don't know!' she told him. 'Yes, my work is part of me, but because it's important to me, not because it's everything.'

'So, we know there's no golf, and you don't put much stock in gourmet dining. What else is there, Caitlin? What other interests do you have?'

She'd have liked to have said reading, which had always been her favoured pastime, but if he asked her what she'd read recently she'd have been stumped, not having picked up a book for months. Or had it been years?

'I like to walk,' she said defiantly, thinking of the pleasure she'd found in walking up the road to the bakery.

'Yet you drive a car that gets you from A to B faster than most vehicles.'

Connor was goading her deliberately, but why?

'I walk when I have time.' Caitlin said the words bluntly, folded her arms across her chest in what she recognised as a classic defensive gesture and turned to stare out the window.

Which was a wasted move, she realised as he pulled up in the hospital car park.

'Like you eat when you have time,' he said softly.

She turned towards him and he reached out and slid his knuckles gently down her cheek. 'Has it been so tough, proving yourself in the scientific field? Have you always had to battle to prove you're as good as any man, or any less beautiful woman?'

His sympathy was so unexpected a lump formed in her throat and threatened to choke her if she spoke. Shaking her head, she tried a smile instead and turned his words into a weapon.

'Now, don't go getting soft on me,' she chided. 'I can fight my own battles and I'll take you on if you get in my way, Connor Clarke, so don't think ''nice'' will change my mind about staying on in Turalla.'

He didn't reply but opened the door. The interior light came on, revealing a smile he hadn't time to wipe away before she saw it.

'OK. I'll try to remember that,' he promised. 'No more Mr Nice Guy, by order of the management.'

She knew he was teasing her—and found herself liking it. Shocked by the discovery, she sprang out of the car before he could come close again. They walked together around the hospital building, dimmed lights gleaming through drawn curtains.

Around the back, the kitchen door was closed. Nellie must have served the supper then gone home. There was a strip of darkness between the large building and her small temporary home and Caitlin was wondering at which point the security lights would come on when something scurried across her feet. She let out an almighty scream and flung herself at Connor.

He caught her body and she felt his strength and warmth—but couldn't stop the uncontrollable trembling in her limbs or still the rapid beating of her heart.

'Hey, it was a cat,' he soothed. 'I think it was intent on stalking some small prey and we startled it.'

'Not as much as it startled me,' she mumbled, and tried to pull away, embarrassed by her reaction—and by letting this man see her stupid fears.

But pulling away wasn't easy. The hands she'd studied earlier were as strong as she'd suspected, and every bit as tender as they smoothed up and down her arms, her back, and kneaded at her neck, lifting the weight of her hair to touch taut skin.

'It's OK to get a fright,' he said quietly, holding her tucked against his body while the fingers of one hand tilted her chin so he could look into her face. 'Shows you're human after all.'

Then his head bent towards her and his lips brushed hers.

'Very human,' he added.

She waited, breath held, for the kiss to develop, for him to finish what he'd begun, but he lifted his head, shook it as if to clear it, then turned her in his arms and guided her towards the house, the light coming on almost immediately.

The harsh glare made her fears seem stupid, and her fantasies even more ridiculous. She stepped away from him, thanked him politely for escorting her home and hurried forward to open the door.

It was the light from outside that caught the gleam of white on the floor, a tiny triangle, nothing more, the bulk of the note or envelope hidden by the mat. Caitlin was about to bend and pick it up, thinking Nellie might have come across with a message, or perhaps Melissa had called, then some instinct stopped the movement and instead she stepped inside, putting her foot over the tell-tale gleam—hiding it from Connor.

She turned on the inside light and glanced around the room. Everything seemed normal.

'Goodnight,' he said, but hovered as if he half expected her to ask him inside.

'Goodnight, and thanks again,' she replied, dashing his hopes. As he moved away, she closed the door and slumped against it.

She looked around the room, realising how little notice she'd taken of it earlier. Last night she'd been too tired, barely registering the polished timber floor, the patterned carpet square, imitation leather lounge chairs.

She lifted her foot and peered down at the tell-tale scrap of white, wondering if it could have been there when she'd arrived. Maybe she wouldn't have noticed it in daylight, the white against the pale polished wood. Or perhaps she'd dislodged it with her foot when she'd been walking out earlier this evening—an old piece of paper left by a previous tenant of the house.

So why didn't she stop wondering, simply bend down and pick it up? Have a look at it instead of guessing?

Because a totally unscientific and irrational sixth sense told her not to—to forget about it and go to bed, to kick it under the mat and let it stay there, out of sight and out of mind.

But would it be? Out of sight perhaps, but not out of mind. With a long sigh she knelt and carefully lifted the edge of the carpet square as if clumsiness might damage what was hidden there. It was a folded piece of paper, with printing and brightly coloured illustrations—a page out of a book of fairy-tales.

She chuckled softly at her fears and unfolded it but the laughter died on her lips as she stared at the picture. It was familiar enough—Sleeping Beauty in her glass case, waiting for the Prince to come and kiss her back to life.

Only in this illustration the glass box looked like a coffin, and the princess's hands were folded on her chest in an attitude of death, not sleep. Then, as if the long golden hair might not be enough of a clue, someone had printed 'Dr O'Shea' very clumsily beneath the drawing, leaving Caitlin in no doubt as to the message.

CHAPTER FIVE

CAITLIN crumpled the piece of paper into a ball and flung it across the room.

'So, someone apart from Connor Clarke doesn't want you in the town.' She said the words aloud, hoping to make them more believable.

It didn't work! Did absolutely nothing to relax the tension in her neck and shoulders, or settle the tumult in her stomach.

She tried to think, use her brain, work out if the piece of paper had been there all along or had been slipped beneath the door while she'd been out that evening.

With security lights coming on and Nellie watching?

But Nellie hadn't been there just now…

Not that discovering when it had come made much difference, she decided. Whenever it had arrived, it sure as hell wasn't a 'good luck' message.

With a puzzled shake of her head and a deep sigh, she headed for her bedroom. She'd sort her preparatory notes into some kind of order—see how Granny's information looked in various graph forms.

But as she reached out to switch on the bedroom light, a nameless terror grabbed her, squeezing air from her lungs and making her knees shake uncontrollably.

'Switch on the light,' she told herself aloud. 'You have to know.'

It took a couple of tries but eventually she did it. The computer was in place, its grey shell gleaming softly, the screen blank but comforting in its blankness. Her relief was instantaneous, propelling her across the room to touch the machine, to pat it as if in comfort.

It was only then she realised her fear had been for it, an inanimate object, not for herself. That the fundamental reaction had been caused not by thoughts of an intruder lurking in the darkness, waiting to harm her in some way, but by the idea of someone messing with her work.

'Which in itself is a reflection of my life,' she muttered, wondering why the thought made her angry when once it would have pleased her.

She booted the machine to action and sat down in front of it, telling herself it was a far better companion than Connor, and more fulfilling than any number of children under five.

Shuddering slightly, she opened the program she wanted and was soon absorbed in her work, spreading names and dates across the screen, manipulating them to see what fitted where. By two o'clock she had generations of the Russell family neatly represented, back as far as great-great-grandparents. She saved the work onto a floppy disk then, remembering her earlier fear, pulled the laptop out from under the bed and transferred the information to its hard disk as well.

It wasn't much, but she was damned if she was going to lose it, she thought as she fell into bed.

Or leave town!

Sleep brought oblivion—no dreams, no recurrence of the nightmares—nothing but blankness until she woke to the aggravating whine of a ride-on mower beyond her window.

It was ten o'clock so she could hardly yell abuse at its operator. In fact, if it wasn't for the noise, she'd have enjoyed the smell of fresh-mown grass.

Ten o'clock? She was seeing Judy Laurence at ten-thirty! Ten minutes to shower and dress, another ten for a much-needed cup of coffee and some sustenance. Which would give her ten minutes to walk to Judy's place. Surely she'd passed Short Street on her way uptown yesterday. There was a map in the file Melissa had left—she'd check it while she ate her cereal. She'd decided, whenever possible, to walk to her appointments, not drive, knowing a sports car could give people a false first impression which she'd then have to battle to overcome.

The map showed she had passed Short Street the previous day and that it was close enough to walk. She made it to Judy's front door with a couple of minutes to spare and was greeted with brisk friendliness by an elegant woman with raven-dark hair swept into a neat French roll.

'Come on in. The kettle's boiling. Will you have tea or coffee?'

She ushered Caitlin into an open, sun-filled family room and waved her towards a cane chair upholstered in shades of aqua, teal and rust. Glass doors overlooked a pool, the colour of the water exactly matching the aqua tone in the cushions. The outside area included a gas barbecue and outdoor table and chairs, the whole made private by the fronds of squat palms.

'What a lovely setting!' Caitlin exclaimed, inwardly startled by her reaction as she rarely took much stock of her surroundings.

Judy seemed pleased, blushing slightly as she returned with a tray bearing a coffee-pot, cups and saucers, and a sinful-looking chocolate mudcake.

'It's really far too ''decorated'' for Turalla, but I've always loved messing about with colour and design, and up here...' The words trailed off into a soft sigh.

'Not much call for interior decorators, huh?' Caitlin asked sympathetically, and Judy laughed.

'None at all,' she said. 'I should have had more kids—or that's what my husband tells me. He's an educated and enlightened member of the male species, or was until we moved up here. Lately he's reverted to an Iron John and seems to think having babies should provide all the fulfilment any woman needs.'

'Since you've been up here?' Caitlin echoed. 'I had the idea you were a local.'

Judy smiled.

'Granny Russell, I suppose! There's no escaping, is there? I was a local, but I left town at sixteen. I couldn't wait to escape to the city.'

'Snap!'

'You, too? A small country town?'

Caitlin nodded.

'Yep, but I stayed on in the city. What's your story?'

Her hostess didn't answer immediately, busying herself pouring coffee, cutting cake, offering a small plate and napkin to Caitlin. It wasn't until she sat back in her chair, her coffee-cup cradled in her hands, that she finally spoke.

'I met a man,' she said softly. 'An engineer with big ideas and even bigger shoulders. He's gorgeous, my Martin, I still think that. I fell in love and knew I'd follow him to the ends of the earth.'

'Or back to Turalla?' Caitlin said softly, feeling the love Judy felt for her man hanging in the room like a lingering perfume.

'Always knew it was the end of the earth!' Judy replied, nodding and smiling at the same time. 'Actually, a return to Turalla was the last thing I expected. I'd thought more of the Middle East, or South America, even New Guinea.'

Her smile broadened. 'Not that I didn't have a taste of those as well. Annabel was born in Rio, and we had two years in the United Arab Emirates.'

'Then back to Turalla?' Caitlin asked. 'It's starting to sound like a song title.'

'Four years ago. We'd only been here a month and, knowing we'd be settled for a while, were even considering having another child. Then Annabel fell ill and...'

'How far into remission is she now?' Caitlin asked, although she knew the answer.

As Judy began to explain, she knew she'd guessed correctly. Parents usually welcomed the opportunity to talk about their child's cancer, yet didn't want to force it on others, so tended to keep it bottled up inside them.

'For so long it was all we thought about,' Judy finished. 'Another baby just wasn't an option.'

'And now?' Caitlin prompted.

'Definitely not! I couldn't go through that again. We were lucky with Annabel as it was caught early and she went into a clean remission after only one treatment, but if it happened again…' She paused, then seemed to gather herself together. 'Even before Anthea Cummings told me you were coming, we'd read where there was a bigger likelihood of siblings contracting the disease. No, Annabel is it for us. We just thank heaven daily that we've still got her.'

Caitlin shivered although her lips were smiling, registering an appropriate reaction to the happiness in Judy's voice. She must be getting fanciful, she decided. First love as an entity in the room, and now a coldness, as if the ghost of Jonah Neil had touched her soul.

'More cake?'

'No, thanks, I know my limits.' She looked at Judy, wondering if she was ready for questions, and caught the other woman smiling at her.

'Ask away,' she encouraged. 'I'm only too pleased to help.'

But someone isn't, Caitlin remembered as she opened up the folder and found the list of questions.

Contrary to Melissa's suggestion, Judy seemed keen to talk about her family's place in the town's history, regaling Caitlin with tales of the wild times on the goldfields, stories passed down through generations of Snapes in the same manner as the original inhabitants of the land kept their history alive.

'Now, can we try to get some order into this?' Caitlin asked, still giggling over Judy's tale of Great-aunt Mildred's bloomers. 'You said Mildred was a Russell— do you know her father's first name?'

She teased out the threads, drawing lines of direct ancestry downwards, noting sideways relationships and diversions on the right, jotting down phone numbers as Judy gave her the names of people who might be able to confirm a possibility or add a pertinent fact.

'Will that help at all?' Judy asked, when Caitlin explained she had to go.

'Enormously,' Caitlin assured her. 'In fact, I'd love to go right home and put it all into the computer, but I've an appointment with Anne Jackson in half an hour so I'd better stick to research today and play with the figures tonight.'

'Anne Jackson handled Harry's illness extremely well,' Judy said, apropos of nothing.

Caitlin looked at her and saw concern in her eyes.

'And now?'

Judy shrugged.

'I really don't know. We were all so close at one stage. Harry was in remission when Annabel was diagnosed and Anne was wonderful, explaining to me what we'd have to go through. Now? She seems to shun the rest of us, as if the sharing brought her into too close an intimacy with us.' She shrugged helplessly. 'She's a nurse at the hospital so you'll have medicine in common. Perhaps she'll talk more freely to you.'

Or perhaps she doesn't want me here, Caitlin thought, remembering the silent message.

'I noticed on Harry's file there's no mention of a Mr. Jackson. Did he die? Or is she divorced?'

Judy looked uncomfortable.

'Anne's never married. Her story is she wanted children, not a husband. She grew up here then went away to do her training and nurse for a while, but no one knows about the children's father—not even if it was the same man,' she explained. 'That's not gossip. I'm telling you because you asked. And because it might make it easier for you when you're talking to her.'

Caitlin smiled.

'Help me from making some unforgivable *faux pas*, you mean?'

'Something like that,' Judy agreed, an answering smile lighting her face. 'Let's keep in touch,' she suggested impulsively. 'We don't have to talk about your work, but it would be nice to see you again—socially. Perhaps lunch?'

'I'd love that,' Caitlin replied, only realising how much she meant it after she'd said goodbye and was walking away. Was it the natural friendliness of a country town getting to her, or was it Connor's jibe about the emptiness of her life?

Anne Jackson lived a block closer to the hospital, in a weatherboard house that seemed to lean into the shadows of the huge mango tree behind it. A jumble of toys decorated the veranda, but the house, when Anne invited her in, was spotless. Not as expensively furnished as Judy's but with a friendly, country-cottage air about it that made Caitlin feel at home.

'Check the chair before you sit down,' Anne warned. 'The kids are supposed to leave their toys on the veranda but that rule works better in theory than in practice. Have you had lunch? I could make you a sandwich.'

She spoke briskly, almost brusquely. Talking to conceal something? No, she seemed welcoming enough.

'I've been gorging on Judy Laurence's mudcake,' Caitlin admitted. 'So no to a sandwich but I wouldn't mind a cup of coffee. I keep promising myself I'll do something about this caffeine addiction—but not just yet.'

Anne smiled and her slightly stern face relaxed.

'Me, too,' she agreed. 'I fell into the trap of drinking it on night duty when I first began nursing and these days it's a four-cup habit to get through the shift.'

'You work night duty at the hospital?' Caitlin asked, hoping her question sounded like natural interest, not hysteria.

'Permanently,' Anne explained. 'Start at eleven. It suits me because I can be with the kids in the afternoon, put them into bed, then be back to have breakfast with them and take them to school. Weekends are a bit hectic if I'm on duty as no matter how hard they try, they really haven't a clue about keeping quiet while I sleep.'

'Kids? How many do you have?'

'Come into the kitchen while I make the coffee,' Anne said, standing up again and leading the way towards the back of the house. 'If we start talking now you'll never get your fix.' She filled an electric kettle then reached for a coffee plunger. 'To answer your question, just the two. I thought you'd have known that from Harry's file.'

Had she walked away deliberately? Caitlin wondered, watching the woman busy herself with the small domestic chore. Had there been another child? Judy's warning echoed in her mind and she resolved to tread warily.

'I probably read it—more than once, in fact—but until I've met everyone it's difficult to keep the names straight in my mind. I know Harry's nine. How old is his sibling? Girl or boy?'

'Rachel's five. She wasn't born when Harry was first diagnosed with cancer. Though now she knows he was ill. I don't know whether the extra attention he had to have will affect her later.'

There was no self-pity in the woman's voice but Caitlin sensed her toughness was a façade to hide a lot of pain.

'Did she go down to the city with you when Harry went for follow-up?' she asked, taking advantage of this opening to explore a little further.

'Of course. Where else should she have been?'

It was an abrupt response, almost abrasive, yet the words seemed more defensive than belligerent, shutting off any chance of further conversation on the subject.

'And you? Are you from this area? I think I explained on the phone about looking for genetic links between the children.'

Anne gave a bark of unmirthful laughter.

'You did, but the story had already spread. Seems

everyone in town knew what you were up to before you'd unpacked your bags. *And* that you'd had dinner with Connor. That started a nice line in gossip, that did.'

Caitlin studied her, wondering if the woman fancied Connor. Could jealousy be behind Anne's attitude? Not that she wasn't welcome to the man. In fact, they'd suit each other—both blew hot and cold.

'Would you prefer not to talk about your family background?' she asked, not wanting to antagonise someone who might have slid a nasty illustration under her mat.

Anne turned slowly, her body tense and her eyes watchful.

Fear brushed along Caitlin's spine, irrational but real.

'It's not that I don't want to talk about it, but I have to know it's confidential. Who's going to see this work of yours? Who's going to know in the end what the family connections are?'

'Myself,' Caitlin told her. 'No one else will ever know as there's no need for it. I'll be using code names—or possibly colours—to represent the different strands of heredity. If common ancestry and genetic heritage is confirmed—and that's a big if—then we'll do some DNA testing. After that, who knows?'

She could feel Anne's interest but knew some internal battle was going on within her.

'You'll want the children's father's line included?' she asked, and Caitlin felt as if a huge hole had opened beneath her feet. What had Connor said about ripples spreading out across a lake? Who knew what they would touch?

'Not if you're not prepared to tell me,' she said. 'I can work off one line, as I'll be doing with children like Annabel whose father isn't a local.'

The silence told her this wasn't the case with Anne's children. Whoever had fathered them was right here in Turalla—or had come from here originally. So why the mystery? And how come no one knew? Towns like this prided themselves on knowing every detail of each other's lives—especially who was going where with whom. Yet Anne Jackson must have pulled off a conjuring trick not once but twice.

'Where did you do your training?' she asked, as a possible solution occurred to her.

'Down in the city,' Anne replied, relaxing slightly and gesturing towards a chair as if they'd both been standing long enough. 'At the Royal, in fact. At least when I had to go down with Harry I had that comfort—I knew my way around the place and had friends still working there.'

Which led naturally into a discussion on Harry's treatment and the doctors' hope that this remission might be permanent. Caitlin noticed she didn't use the word 'cured'.

'And your family? Have you relatives in town?' she asked, and Anne laughed.

'More than you can poke a stick at,' she said. 'Like the Russells, we're related to just about everyone and while that's a curse when you're growing up, I couldn't have coped without my immediate family. Mum's been wonderful and one or other of my relatives sleep over so I can go to work. These days it's my youngest sister. She's sixteen and still at high school. When she goes off to university, I'll have a niece old enough to take over from her.'

She sighed, then added, 'Yes, I couldn't manage without family, no matter how irritating they are at times!'

'Organising your life? Making suggestions—but always for your own good?' Caitlin asked, smiling her understanding of the problem.

'Exactly!'

Anne smiled back, a natural, friendly smile—and Caitlin saw how attractive she was when the woman allowed herself to relax. Was the children's father still around? Was that why she'd stayed single?

'And speaking of families, aren't there questions you want to ask?'

Anne's words jerked her back to work-related matters. The woman's love life was none of her business.

'Plenty,' she agreed. 'We'll start with your family and go back—parents, grandparents, great-grandparents if you know of them—as far back as possible. Then later I'd like to know about your siblings and their families. What I'm hoping to end up with is a bunch of kids with similar bloodlines, some of whom did get leukaemia and some who didn't.'

'Then you'll do DNA testing and try to find out why?' Anne asked.

'Exactly,' Caitlin agreed, but as Anne reached for a writing pad and ballpoint pen, Caitlin knew she'd lost her—that the tenuous thread of friendship they'd established with talk of country towns and families had been snapped.

Anne had pulled back from her. But why?

She watched Anne scribble names on the paper, representing her family with a traditional 'tree'.

'There,' Anne said, pushing her diagrammatic explanation towards Caitlin. 'I've left blanks where I don't know things. I've more information about Mum's family than Dad's. He's related to the Russells but I think there's a mix of generations there somewhere. Granny was the youngest of a large family and her older sister was having babies before Granny was born, so you could get confused there.'

She was being helpful. Too helpful? Caitlin studied the names.

'This is great,' she said, hoping a little enthusiasm might re-establish the earlier rapport.

'Good!' Anne replied, then she looked at her watch and stood up. 'I have to go up to the school to collect the kids,' she said.

So much for rapport! Caitlin stuck the sheet of paper in her file and followed Anne towards the front veranda.

'You've other people to see?' Anne called to her, when they'd said goodbye and Caitlin was walking down the front path towards the gate.

She turned towards the house.

'Yes, and then plenty of work to do, putting it all together,' she agreed, but Anne's frowning face told her the woman had something on her mind. Was she worried Caitlin would press her for Harry's father's details—or feeling guilty because she didn't want to reveal them? 'I'll let you know how it's going if you like.'

Anne shrugged, as if the outcome of Caitlin's work held little interest for her, but Caitlin had sensed her fear when she'd spoken of Harry's illness—a fear not for her son but for her daughter who shared his bloodlines. With her medical background she'd understood what Caitlin was trying to do—and also how important that work might be for Rachel's future. Yet, for the work to be complete, she would have to reveal the name of the children's father—a secret she'd kept successfully for at least nine years.

As Caitlin walked away, she wondered about Anne's lover. Were they still involved with each other? Could she turn to him with her doubts and questions, talk her dilemma through with him? Or had he cut himself off from them? Perhaps been in the city at the same time she'd been studying, then left her for someone else?

But that was hardly likely, given the gap in ages between the children!

And now? Was Anne looking for another man? Someone to act as a father to her children, to provide her with companionship—with love?

And why should she need love any more than you do? Caitlin demanded of herself. Then she sighed, for her scornful question lacked its usual zest, and she wondered if perhaps she did need love.

Quickening her pace as if she might outdistance her

thoughts, Caitlin turned her mind from love to mental shopping lists. In spite of what she'd said to Connor, there was a limit to how long she could exist on bread and breakfast cereal—particularly now she'd run out of milk.

She had her list complete by the time she reached the hospital and decided she'd drop off her notes at the house then drive up town to the supermarket. Mike Nelson interrupted these plans, once again calling to her from the front veranda of the hospital.

'Do you lie in wait for me or do you keep watch on everyone approaching the place? Surely an axe murderer intent on doing away with your patients would creep around the back?'

He grinned at her and motioned for her to come up the steps.

'Nellie keeps watch at the back,' he pointed out. 'Actually, I was heading back to my office and saw you coming this way. Decided it was time you had the guided tour. Come along.'

He led the way into the building, passing his office on the left and taking the next door on that side.

'You came in to see Granny, so saw the rooms down that side. Along this corridor is the emergency room— what used to be A and E until we became Americanised— then a small treatment room, and next to that the theatre.'

'For an older building, it's remarkably well laid out,' Caitlin said, appreciating how services like X-ray and pathology had been clustered near these suites for efficiency.

Mike beamed at her.

'Thanks—that's partly my doing. When the Health Department started talking about building a new hospital, I told them it was a shame to pull down a building that worked, so their planners came up and together we nutted out what needed to be renovated.'

They walked through the wing that housed the hostel then he led her into the kitchen—behind the yellow line that divided off the food preparation area.

'Here, too, we just altered things so the food preparation area is classed as a restricted area—see Nellie's gown and slippers—but staff can come in here, even sit at the table like they did in the old days, and have a cup of coffee and talk to Nellie, who stays on the other side of the table.'

It seemed a good compromise to Caitlin, who'd sat at a similar table in the kitchen of the hospital in her old home town, being spoilt with goodies from the cook.

Mike departed, leaving Caitlin with Nellie who pressed a plate of freshly cooked scones on her and offered to prepare Caitlin's evening meals.

'There's a proper dining room just across the hall,' she said, nodding towards the door. 'And a book in there. You just write down what time you'll be in for a meal, and I'll have it ready for you. That's if you don't want to come in here.

'Saves you doing any shopping,' Nellie continued. 'I know about cooking in temporary quarters—doesn't matter what you choose to make, there's always one ingredient you don't have.'

'I suppose you're right,' Caitlin responded, unwilling to admit that her 'cooking' rarely required ingredients. She steamed or stir-fried vegetables and usually grilled her meat, fish or chicken, a little pepper and a dash of soy sauce her only condiments. 'But I'm better being independent. It's hard to know when I'll be wanting meals.'

Nellie seemed unfazed by her decision.

'Suit yourself, but any time you're feeling hungry at about seven, there'll be food in here—and company.'

Was that it? Caitlin wondered as she crossed the yard between the hospital and house. Did Nellie want to talk to her? As company, or for some other reason?

Mike had explained that the domestic staff, including a kitchen hand who did the heavy work for Nellie, all finished by five—some earlier. One wardsman was on duty at night to assist the nursing staff should moving a patient be necessary, and he helped the aides serve the meals. The wardsman also acted as the X-ray technician and a general gofer for the nurses.

So he'd be in the wards, or the small staffroom, she assumed, and Nellie would be on her own until supper was over and she could go home.

OK, so I'll go over and have dinner with Nellie one night, Caitlin decided. But not tonight!

She'd reached her front door and hesitated before reaching out to open it.

Don't be silly, she chided herself, clutching the doorknob and turning it firmly.

It moved obligingly but when she pushed against it, the door refused to budge.

She rattled the doorknob and tried again, kicked the lower panel and had another go—then remembered Connor talking about keys! Someone had locked the place.

With a weary sigh she turned back towards the kitchen.

'I can't get into my house,' she complained to Nellie, who laughed delightedly then reached into the capacious pocket of her apron.

'Forgot to tell you. Connor found a key. He locked the place and told me to give you this.'

She handed Caitlin a long, old-fashioned-looking black metal key.

'We used to have keys like that at home. Same one opens every door in the house—even opened our next-door neighbours' place as well.'

Caitlin added her thanks then retraced her steps to her front door. Now they'd limited the people who could get into her place to those who lived in the older houses or happened to have a key that fitted.

Like Anne Jackson?

She shook her head to clear the thought. It was ridiculous. Anne was defensive because of her situation—but to wish harm to another woman?

The key worked, and a cursory glance around the place failed to reveal any new message of disaster.

Great! Shopping first then back to work. Or perhaps a little work…

She could feel her fingertips buzzing with an urgency to key in the new information, and it was only the thought of having to pour water on her cereal in the morning that won the inner battle.

By six o'clock her groceries had been put away and she'd cooked and eaten a plate of vegetables, so she could work through for a few hours without having to stop for a proper meal. Later, she'd take a break—perhaps at ten—and have some supper then.

She smiled at this evidence of order and domesticity and finally allowed herself to settle in front of the computer screen.

Her excitement grew as she added more and more names to her 'tree'. The families were meshing and intertwining, and her fingers flew across the keys, issuing commands, demanding new configurations of the information, tying the threads of relationship from one family to the next.

At some stage she'd heard an ambulance, its screaming siren cutting through the night air like the cry of an animal in pain. Work for Connor, her brain had registered, but she'd not been diverted long, her mind too focussed on the emerging pattern.

She heard the knocking but it took a minute for its meaning to register. Pushing reluctantly away from the computer, she straightened up, grimacing as muscles that had been inactive for too long protested at the movement.

A nurse she hadn't met stood outside, looking worried and distracted.

'Connor said could you come. It's a—' The young woman broke off then tried again. 'It's a…'

She burst into tears.

CHAPTER SIX

WHATEVER it was, it was urgent, Caitlin realised, putting an arm around the nurse's shoulders, making soothing noises, but leading her straight back to the hospital.

'Get yourself a cup of tea,' she told the nurse, abandoning her near the kitchen. Then, putting together urgency and the ambulance siren, Caitlin made her way to the emergency room Mike had shown her earlier.

Anne and Connor were bent over a patient near the door. Perhaps hearing her approach, Connor looked up.

'MVA. Could you check that lad?' he asked, nodding to the second bed in the small room. 'Mike's on his way in.'

MVA—motor vehicle accident—the same shorthand was used in emergency departments all over the country.

'Come on, damn you, live!' Connor was muttering at his patient as Caitlin pulled a curtain around the second bed.

She picked up the transfer papers from the ambulance and the file the upset nurse must have started. Warwick Bell, aged seventeen. Concussion. Lower limb damage. The rest of the information on the sheet was sketchy and Caitlin realised the ambulance attendants' attention had been centred on the more seriously injured occupant of the car—the young man Connor was willing back to life.

Caitlin concentrated on Warwick. He was unconscious and had an oxygen mask over his mouth and nose but no tube in place so presumably his airway was clear. His neck was protected by a cervical collar and a short spine board was still strapped around his torso. She picked up the stethoscope that hung above the bed and listened to his chest. Once Mike arrived they could use an oximeter to check oxygen saturation in his blood.

Blood next—no bad external bleeding, though he had blood seeping from scrapes and cuts on his face and a bandage on his left forearm which she assumed covered a flesh injury. His blood pressure was good, pulse a little fast. She checked his injured leg, noticing the swelling below the knee, and stripped off his right shoe and sock, seeking a peripheral pulse in his foot. It was there, faint but noticeable, so she knew blood was still getting through.

She slid a catheter into the back of his left hand, knowing fluids could be needed urgently if his condition deteriorated, took a vial of blood for typing and testing, then moved on.

Through the curtain, she could hear Connor talking, entreating his patient to stay alive. The clatter of instruments, the murmured conversation between Anne and Connor suggested it was an epic battle and Caitlin felt her chest grow tight as she wondered if they'd win.

But she had her own patient to tend. Head next. She was talking to him all the time, and now she asked him to open his eyes. To her surprise, his eyelids flickered and with only a little further encouragement, he managed the task. Blue eyes, as clear as a baby's but empty of any understanding. His pupils were dilated but even in size, and responded when she shone a torch into them. She kept talking to him, seeking a response to voice commands. He moved a finger when asked, but didn't respond verbally, though he was obviously aware of his pain, groaning as Caitlin touched his body.

'Warwick, speak to me, tell me how you feel.'

The blue eyes focussed this time, and one word—'Lousy'—made Caitlin feel better. That one word, though it came out a bit garbled, told her Warwick's level of unconsciousness was not as great as she'd feared.

Mike arrived as she was noting her assessment of her

patient on the chart, classing him as thirteen on the Glasgow coma scale, where severe injury started at eleven and coma with a score of seven or less.

'Hell, it's Warwick! Where's Kirstie?'

Caitlin looked blankly at the new arrival.

'The nurse who was on duty—covering Emergency. Slight build, blonde hair.'

Caitlin recognised the description of the nurse who'd come to get her, and explained to Mike she'd left her near the kitchen.

'Are you OK here for another few minutes?' Mike asked, and Caitlin, who was surprised to find how much of her training was coming back to her, nodded.

'I'll have to find her,' Mike explained. 'Warwick's her brother.'

Left on her own, Caitlin first repeated the check of her patient's vital signs—still good—then turned her attention to a secondary survey. Warwick was moving now as full consciousness returned, lifting his arms to try to orientate himself. He moved his left, less injured leg on command, which reassured Caitlin about spinal injury.

She unstrapped the spine board but left it where it was until Mike returned to help her remove it. Took off Warwick's other shoe and sock, then cut off his torn and blood-stained jeans.

'Hey, they're good,' he protested, but as she'd found a deep, soft tissue wound on his left thigh and was swabbing it clean, the protest died in another cry, this one of pain.

She worked her way carefully over his body, cleaning bits of dirt out of contusions, putting fresh dressings on his arm, tending all the superficial wounds.

Mike returned.

'One of the other nurses on duty is taking care of Kirstie,' he told Caitlin. 'So, what next?'

'X-ray.'

'OK.'

A fluent string of oaths from beyond the curtain had them both glancing that way.

'Bad?' Mike asked, and Caitlin nodded.

'I think so,' she said quietly.

She and Mike wheeled Warwick through to X-Ray, where, with the help of the wardsman, they shifted Warwick onto the X-ray table.

'We'll manage this part,' Mike told her. 'What do you want?'

'Right leg for sure, then head and neck as precautionary measures. According to the transfer papers, he was wearing a seat belt but there could be indications of whiplash.'

Mike nodded, and Caitlin left them to it, returning to the emergency room and the patient Connor had been swearing over.

Anne was gone, and Connor was bent over the bed. He straightened and turned as he heard Caitlin approach.

'We lost him,' he said, ashen-faced with defeat. 'Stupid, stupid boy, out there speeding and no seat belt. Massive head and chest injuries. His parents are here. I'll have to talk to them.'

He walked past Caitlin and down the corridor, his usually straight shoulders bowed.

Uncertain what to do next, Caitlin waited, then Anne returned with a sheaf of papers in her hand.

'Always paperwork,' she said, the bitterness of defeat in her voice, too.

'Can I do something?' Caitlin asked.

Anne shrugged, then perched on a stool, glanced at the clock and bent her head over the forms.

Mike returned. 'Connor's seen the films. Head's OK but there's a bad fracture of the fibula. Must have been the way he was sitting in the car. The flying surgeon comes tomorrow, so we'll leave the leg until then. Connor's ordered a drip and some pain relief, and said we can put Warwick to bed. Thanks for your help, Caitlin. We really appreciate it.'

Thus dismissed, Caitlin made her way back to her temporary home, feeling flat and somehow dissatisfied.

Even the computer failed to lure her, though hunger finally asserted itself and she flicked on the kitchen light and considered her options. Nice to have options! Toast perhaps, with peanut butter and honey—that should cover a few of the basic nutritional groups. And a cup of tea—given the late hour and the likelihood that she'd soon be heading for bed.

But she didn't head to bed, too unsettled by the evening's activities. She took the tea and toast into the bedroom and settled in front of the computer again.

She was wondering why the threads of relationships coming together on the machine failed to thrill her when the security lights came on, dazzling her eyes as their brightness flooded the bedroom. A soft tap on the door announced her visitor, and she opened it to see Connor standing there, his hair ruffled, his face still etched with strain.

'Saw your light on and thought I'd pop in,' he said lightly, trying a smile but failing so dismally she wanted to put her arms around him and give him a hug.

'I've just made tea. Want some? And toast? Or I've got some scones.'

Caitlin took his hand and tugged him in. As she reached behind him to shut the door, the outside lights went out, and in the sudden darkness she saw a movement in the shadows on the hospital veranda—a flash of white as if someone had stood there watching, then moved away as the door began to close.

One of the night staff grabbing some fresh air, she told herself, more concerned with her visitor than the unknown person on the veranda.

'Sit down,' she said to Connor. 'I assume you've just been talking to the parents. That has to be the crappiest job in all of medicine.'

He shrugged his shoulders then rubbed his hand through his hair, completing the disarray.

'You could say that!' he muttered, then he looked around as if uncertain of his whereabouts. 'I should go home. Shouldn't be bothering you…'

The words trailed into nothingness and Caitlin took his hand again, but this time she turned him towards her so she could look into his face.

'Talk about it,' she suggested, as his despair washed over her as well. 'Talk to me. It won't hurt and it often helps. You know that, Connor. It's not the first time.'

He nodded, and she took him in her arms and drew his body close to hers, offering a comfort as old as time itself. 'Stupid young fool!' he said, pressing the words against her hair. 'Why won't kids learn? Why, when they see the graphic horror of road accidents on TV, do they still believe they're invincible?'

There wasn't any answer, so she stayed silent, just holding him and hoping that would help.

'God, I feel so useless when that happens, Caitlin. I wonder how far medicine has come when we still lose strong young men.'

He brushed his lips against her forehead, a kiss that wasn't really a kiss.

'It isn't medicine that fails them,' she murmured. 'Young men have always sought thrills to test themselves and the ultimate thrill is pitting yourself against your fear. Why else did they go so willingly to war—right down through the ages? OK, some were conscripted—forced to go—but most went willingly, seeing only the adventure and the challenge, not the grisly, ugly reality of death. And no matter how far medical skills improve, you can't fix bodies broken or torn beyond repair.'

She could feel the tension easing in his body but it wasn't his body she should be concerned about now. It was her own, responding to his in a most unprofessional— most uncomforting—way. Her heart was skidding about beneath her ribs and her lips pricking with a memory of that light and casual kiss he'd dropped on them last night.

'Tea and toast?' she offered again, using the offer as an excuse to step away from him.

He shook his head.

'I couldn't eat. And shouldn't it be tea and sympathy?' This smile was slightly better—rueful, but with a hint of humour that was echoed in his eyes. 'I shouldn't have come and dumped on you like this. I'm—'

Caitlin closed in on him again, reaching up to put her fingers on his lips.

'If you say you're sorry I'm likely to do you an injury. Can't you see I'm glad you came to me? It means, for all your scoffing at my life, you must see glimpses of a person beneath the computerised scientist.'

'Tantalising glimpses,' he agreed, taking her hand in his and gently kissing the palm. 'Thank you for listening. And thanks for coming to the rescue earlier. Kirstie's a good nurse and would have coped, but when I saw it was Warwick, I knew I couldn't ask it of her.'

He sighed, and slumped down on one of the stools at the breakfast bar.

'It's one of the curses of small-town life,' he said. 'The patient is nearly always someone you know, and when there's a death, it affects everyone.'

'But one of the plusses,' Caitlin reminded him, 'is that support systems swing automatically into place. There'll be friends and family waiting for the parents of the young man who died when they get home. There'll be people to lean on, and listen, and help in whatever way that family needs.'

Connor managed a tired smile.

'You're right,' he said, then shrugged again. 'Makes it hard to be an outsider.'

It was a strange comment, but Caitlin knew what he meant. The family would have someone to lean on, but when he went home he'd be alone.

But even as this thought surfaced she realised he'd shaken off the melancholy and was strongly in control again.

'I'd better be off. I need to check on Warwick and have a talk to Anne before I head for home.'

Connor was out the door, and the security lights had come on again, before he turned and faced her with a now-familiar frown drawing his dark brows together.

'That door wasn't locked!' he muttered accusingly at her. 'I knocked and then you opened it. I didn't hear a key turn in the lock.'

She wanted to smile, to laugh at his protectiveness, but his scowl suggested he was really angry and, considering he didn't know about the illustration, laughter might be inappropriate.

'I'm sorry,' she said. 'I'll lock it now and try to remember in future.'

The scowl faded and was replaced by a smile. Not quite the full thousand-watt effort, but devastating enough to send her heartbeat into overdrive.

'You see you do,' he ordered.

Caitlin said goodnight and shut the door but she couldn't shut out the memory of that smile, or the thoughts it prompted. Why was such an attractive man still single? And, given that he was, why wasn't someone up here pursuing him?

Perhaps someone was. Would that explain the watcher on the veranda?

Word had got around that she'd had dinner at Connor's on Tuesday night. Anne Jackson had mentioned it. She was also single and possibly in the market for a husband.

And she worked nights.

Caitlin locked the door.

Friday's first appointment was with Robyn Wilson, and as Caitlin scribbled down the information on her husband's family, which Robyn gave willingly, she could feel her excitement stirring. Even without her diagrams, she now knew that three of the children had great-grandparents who were siblings. The relationships between the families, removed to distant cousins over four generations, were not obvious, the most common comment being, 'Oh, we're related to so-and-so a long way back.'

'Have you seen Anthea Cummings?' Robyn asked, when they'd gone back as far as her memory would allow. 'At one time she was interested in doing their family tree. Her husband's family has farmed here since for ever, but I think her folks were from out of town.'

'I spoke to her when she was down for Lucy's treatment but haven't gone into the relationship business with her. I'm driving out to Malawa this afternoon.'

'Great!' Robyn responded, and Caitlin must have looked surprised by her enthusiasm for she added, 'It would be good to have some answers. And even if you don't come up with answers, to have something else crossed off the list. I know about the statistical stuff and realise Aaron could have been one of the unlucky ones who got it anyway, but the fact that so many did, in such a small town, makes it…eerie, somehow.'

'I can understand that and I'm grateful to you all for your help and co-operation. You must be sick of answering questions when no one can give you answers to yours. I thought you might have been more wary about my work, more concerned about the effect it might have on the town.'

'Because of what happened before?' Robyn asked. 'No way! We all welcomed the last lot of experts—that's "we", the parents of the children—and most of the townsfolk did as well. It was only a few old die-hards who caused trouble, seeing it as an opportunity to settle old scores. Have you talked to the Neils?'

The question, riding on the heels of the other matter, made Caitlin pause.

'I've been leaving them to last,' she said. 'The death of a child leaves such a gaping hole in people's lives, I know I'll have to tread carefully.'

Robyn chuckled. 'In more ways than one,' she offered. 'They're a strange couple, keep to themselves. In fact, I used to wonder if Mrs Neil had taken some kind of vow of silence, it was so hard to prise a word out of her. After Lucy, who was the last, was diagnosed, the parent group became almost official, if you know what I mean. The rest of us had been meeting together for support, but with Lucy, Judy Laurence decided something must be done to find out why this was happening. She and I went out to see Mrs Neil, but she refused to speak to us at all. I suppose the fact that we all still call her Mrs Neil tells the story.'

'And Mr Neil?'

'The prophet Ezra?' Robyn smiled. 'He's a strange man. I sometimes wondered if he might be abusive, and that's why Mrs Neil refused to talk to us. Because he'd forbidden it.'

'Are there any signs of abuse that you know of—apart from Mrs Neil's silence?'

Robyn shook her head.

'None at all, and as she works at the hospital, if there were, someone would have noticed for sure. But abuse can be emotional as well as physical, can't it?'

Caitlin agreed. 'But surely, if he's a religious man, abuse would be against his beliefs.'

'Unfortunately I've never listened to him for long enough to know much of his beliefs, although he seems to favour sermons of doom and disaster. I know when the kids got sick we joked about whether he'd foretold the scourge, but when Jonah died the joking stopped. He's been preaching since he dropped out of university and came back to town, years ago.'

'I hadn't realise he actually preached,' Caitlin said. 'From the way Connor—or was it Melissa?—spoke, I thought he was a hermit, completely withdrawn from the life of the town.'

'Every day but Sunday,' Robyn pointed out. 'On Sundays he spreads the word—in the park if there's a market on, on the street corner outside the hotel, even at the hospital if the pub's having a bad day. He likes to know there are a few people around.'

'So even if most of his words fall on deaf ears, there's a chance one sinner might be saved.'

'I guess that's it,' Robyn agreed dubiously. 'I must say I've always just assumed he likes the sound of his own voice. He's the town eccentric, if you like. Small towns always tolerate their own.'

'Their own? Is he a local? For some reason I'd thought of the Neils as newcomers.'

Robyn frowned.

'I've no idea where Mrs Neil came from, but Ezra grew up here—he and Jerry were twins. Jerry had been named Jeremiah, but he was the family rebel and he wouldn't answer to anything but Jerry. He left town a long time ago and the rumour was he got into a lot of trouble. The two of them were quite a few years ahead of me at school. The family may have come from somewhere else originally—beyond planet earth, perhaps—but I've always considered Ezra a local. I'll ask my mother, or Granny Russell would know. Ask her.'

Caitlin considered this. 'Well, I'd prefer to ask Ezra himself, but I guess I'd better tread warily. I'll tackle Granny first.'

She chatted to Robyn for a while longer then left, trying to damp down the flicker of hope that maybe this time she'd come across a clue that might kickstart her new research.

If Ezra Neil *was* a local, there was a chance all the children could be linked together. It would be a beginning, the first step on a long path that might or might not prove useful in the long run.

Leaving Robyn's place, Caitlin considered her next move. She had a few hours to fill in before driving out to Malawa. Mrs Neil worked at the hospital. Should she try to talk to her there? Or ask Granny Russell what she wanted to know?

No, she'd keep that line of action in reserve. Up to now, she'd only questioned parents about their own families—Mrs Neil deserved that much consideration. Caitlin hurried towards the hospital, her mind sorting through all she'd heard and seen and experienced. Was there any significance in three of the families living within walking distance of the hospital, when the new estate where Mike and Sue lived would surely be a more pleasant environment for children? Probably coincidence—a phenomenon all scientists knew had to be taken into consideration.

She sighed, knowing the relationships could prove just as coincidental.

'But I've got to find out,' she told herself firmly, marching with renewed determination towards the hospital steps.

A deep chuckle made her glance up and she saw, not Mike this time but Connor standing there.

'And to think I thought you only talked to your computer,' he teased, smiling down at her in a manner that made her head whirl and her body remember how his had felt when she'd held him in her arms.

Caitlin tried to say hello, or something equally inane, but words refused to come. Tongue-tied by the realisation that what she felt was attraction—but it had never worked this way for her before. And definitely not this suddenly...

Neither would her feet move, she discovered as she tried to act normal—well, not until she gave a very firm order and commanded them to rise and fall.

Up the steps, closer to the man who was causing her so much internal trouble, battling to think of something sensible to say—something work-orientated if possible, so she at least sounded normal.

'Does Mrs Neil work today? Do you think Mike would mind if I spoke to her for a few minutes?'

The smile disappeared as his face clouded over—smile to scowl in a split second.

'Can't you get enough information without bothering the Neils?' he demanded.

'You know I can't,' she snapped, more annoyed with her body which seemed to find even a scowling Connor attractive. 'What kind of scientific hypothesis could I present with incomplete information? I'd be laughed out of my job.'

She glared at him, her anger rising. 'Or is that what you want? Are you so concerned about this town you'd rather see me fail? Well, I'll tell you something, Connor Clarke, so far you're the only one who's shown the slightest hesitation about me being here. Everywhere but here I've been welcomed, so don't go spouting your opinions about what the town wants or doesn't want. By your own admission, you're an outsider looking in.'

Connor wondered how being angry could make Caitlin even more attractive. He found it hard to concentrate on her words when his mind was occupied by the way the colour fluctuated in her cheeks, heat glowing beneath her skin like the red bulb of a torch shone through fine cream-coloured silk.

Should he forget the irrational doubts he'd had, and help her with her quest? Wouldn't it be worth it, if only to see her smile as she'd smiled at him earlier? They could work together, getting to know each other, and he'd find opportunities to touch her, to hold her hand and maybe take her in his arms again.

He remembered the feel of her body pressed against his when she'd offered him comfort the previous evening, and felt his body tighten in response.

'Well?' she demanded, and he tried to remember what they'd been talking about before he'd been distracted by the colour in her cheeks.

Couldn't recall a single word.

'Well, what?' he tried, then knew immediately he'd made the wrong move.

'Well, nothing,' she stormed, and pushed past him, giving a perfunctory knock on Mike's door then going in. And closing it behind her!

Lot of good that would do, he thought, grinning to himself. The window was open and he was two feet from it. But when he heard her greeting Mike he knew he couldn't eavesdrop. He walked away, wondering how to make up the ground he'd lost.

'Morning, Mrs Neil.'

The greeting was automatic, and it triggered his errant memory. That's where the conversation had begun—with Mrs Neil. He spun around, wondering where she'd gone, then walked back to the front door and checked the veranda. He'd opted not to eavesdrop on Mike's and Caitlin's conversation, but would Mrs Neil make the same choice if she heard her name mentioned?

The veranda was deserted. Wherever Mrs Neil had gone, it wasn't to listen outside Mike's window.

He should have been relieved, but remembering why they'd argued brought back his misgivings about the research—and in particular about probing into this one family's background.

As he headed towards his own office, he tried to analyse his reservations. He'd never had a conversation with Ezra Neil, but had met him briefly one Sunday when Ezra had been visiting a patient. Since that occasion, he'd caught glimpses of him quite often, in his old beat-up truck when he collected his wife from her work at the hospital, or speaking on a street corner or the front veranda of the hospital on the Sabbath.

So the man had a big black bushy beard! Was that reason enough to treat him with suspicion?

No, but he'd been the one who'd found Angie's car...

So what? Surely if he'd been in any way involved in Angie's disappearance, he *wouldn't* have found the car…

Connor shook his head, knowing he was in danger of tripping over his own thoughts. Knowing also that it was Mrs Neil's cowed silence that made him suspicious of Ezra. Mrs Neil struck him as a woman very much in awe of her husband. Was the awe fear-related?

'That's where I stick,' he muttered to himself, then he smiled, realising he was guilty of the charge he'd levelled at Caitlin earlier—talking to himself.

'But I speak to most of the inanimate objects in my house,' he added under his breath in case anyone was close enough to hear the conversation. 'Not just a computer.'

Caitlin thanked Mike for his help and headed off in search of Mrs Neil. She ran her to earth in the kitchen, silently swabbing the floor around the stoves with a mop while Nellie sat on a stool, her feet propped on a chair, and carried on a one-sided conversation.

One glance at Mrs Neil's pursed lips told Caitlin this was not the moment to suggest a chat. She greeted Nellie, said no to lunch—'I've still got your scones to eat'—then nodded towards the other woman who had progressed to a far corner.

Nellie got the message.

'Have you met Mrs Neil, Doctor?' she asked. 'You've been in and out so much, I don't know who you know or don't know.'

She smiled at Caitlin, as if to apologise for the fact that Mrs Neil hadn't turned to face them and obviously had no intention of acknowledging any introduction.

Nellie introduced them anyway, but Caitlin could hardly walk across the wet floor to offer her hand so had to make do with a polite remark—delivered to the woman's back.

'She's not one for a chat,' Nellie explained in a whisper that could have been heard uptown, 'but the best worker this hospital has ever had, bar none. And I should know, I've been here going on forty years.'

Caitlin knew she was supposed to show amazement, but if she couldn't talk to Mrs Neil, she'd like to get the new lines drawn into her web of relationships.

'I've got an appointment shortly,' she said to Nellie. 'I'll call in this evening, or see you tomorrow. Or do you not work weekends?'

To Caitlin's surprise it was Mrs Neil who replied.

'Course she works weekends—what else is there for her to do with no man in her life?'

The words were spiteful in content but delivered so flatly Caitlin wondered if she'd meant them to hurt Nellie or had simply been stating a fact.

Whatever the intention, Nellie looked chastened, and Caitlin hurried to her defence.

'Plenty of women don't need a man to make their lives complete,' she argued. 'Including me!'

The last words were defiant, partly to soothe Nellie and partly to reassure herself—seeing 'herself' seemed increasingly confused about the issue.

Mrs Neil made a noise that sounded remarkably like a snort, then opened the door to the pantry and followed her mop inside.

'I'll see you later,' Caitlin told Nellie, heading for the door before the other woman reappeared. Maybe she would ask Granny about the Neils and save herself some aggravation.

She unlocked her door and her heart stopped when she saw the folded note that had been shoved underneath.

Surely not another warning of some kind?

Her knees trembled as she knelt to pick it up, her fingers shook as she lifted it.

This is nonsense, she told herself, setting it unopened on the breakfast bar, and put on the kettle for a cup of coffee. It's a message. Mike, or his admin assistant, had brought it over. They could hardly leave it outside.

But she couldn't bring herself to open it—not until the coffee was made, a scone buttered and she was seated on a stool with her snack set neatly in front of her.

It *was* a message, and it *was* from admin, saying simply that Mrs Cummings had phoned to say she wouldn't be available today. Would Caitlin please phone and arrange another time?

'When Caitlin's nerves have recovered!' she muttered to herself, then she laughed at how easily she'd been spooked and resolved to put the nonsense of the first note completely out of her head.

'After all,' she told herself, 'that first note might have been a compliment. Someone thought you looked like the illustration and wanted you to see it. The coffin and attitude of death was in your mind, not in the picture.'

She ate her scone and drank the coffee. With this afternoon's appointment cancelled, she could get stuck into some real work.

CHAPTER SEVEN

A SUDDEN feeling of emptiness distracted Caitlin from the computer screen. The clock showed seven-fifteen. It had been a long time since she'd had that snack.

Her work was progressing well—she refused to acknowledge it might be going much better than that—with family lines falling into place in a most satisfactory manner. Perhaps, rather than cook, she'd go across and have dinner in the hospital kitchen and get Nellie's views on her presence in the town. She might also mention Mrs Neil—if Nellie had worked at the hospital for forty years, she must know as much about what went on in the town as Granny Russell.

Shower first, clean clothes, do something with her hair, which was hanging limply around her shoulders—yes, a break was what she needed.

What she hadn't needed was the sight of Connor, already settled at the wide kitchen table, head propped contentedly on his elbows as he watched Nellie ladle aromatic meat and vegetables from a large casserole dish.

He turned as the screen door banged behind her and she saw a smile hesitate at the corners of his mouth. His gaze swept over her, taking in the rather amateurish knot she'd made of her hair, fixing it on top of her head with pins, the pale pink lipstick she'd brushed on at the last minute and the gauzy summer dress that swept down to her ankles. A top-to-bottom scrutiny, repeated in reverse until his eyes met hers and the smile stopped hesitating.

'Well, I'm glad to see one of your guests dressed for dinner, Nellie,' he said, and Caitlin realised he was still in his white coat—crumpled and slightly stained by Betadine, his stethoscope dragging at one pocket.

'You coming to eat with us?' Nellie asked.

'Sure am, if that's OK,' Caitlin told her. 'I didn't write my name in the book.'

Nellie waved a hand as if it was unimportant, and Caitlin turned to Connor.

'Had a long day?'

'The longest,' he said, standing up and pulling out a chair for her in a gesture that made her feel both special and foolish. In the cash-strapped lab where she worked, you fought the men for use of stools as well as project funding. She wasn't used to chivalry.

He settled back in his chair and sniffed appreciatively at the dinner Nellie set in front of him.

'Flying surgeon comes once a month. It's much easier for the patients if we can do routine surgery here. Sending them to a larger town for hospitalisation dislocates the family and isolates the patient. Here, friends can visit, relatives don't have to reorganise their lives so someone can accompany the patient out of town—a host of things.'

'And today was the day? I remember Mike mentioning it last night.' Caitlin turned to thank Nellie as her dinner was placed on the table.

'Today was the day,' Connor confirmed. 'All fourteen hours of it! I was taking a breather when I saw you earlier. We're usually better organised, one major op—perhaps a hip or knee replacement—and a few minor things—tonsillectomies, hand contractures or perhaps a carpal tunnel operation, bunions—routine stuff.'

'And today?'

He smiled again and she forgot her hunger as she bathed in the special warmth of that smile. Or was it a heating in her blood supplying the warmth?

'Today we had the aftermath of last night's accident. Young Warwick. It was more complicated than I'd thought, and he's ended up in traction. We were in theatre four hours with him, then had our normal caseload.'

'We?' Caitlin queried.

'I usually play anaesthetist,' he said. 'The government makes sure we have sufficient skills to do the job and provides in-service training especially geared to the needs of rural medicine. But for Warwick's leg, the surgeon needed a hand so Penny, one of our sisters, did the anaesthetic and I assisted, then took over the anaesthetist's job for the others.'

'That kind of day coming on top of last night—it's no wonder you're tired,' Caitlin sympathised, and won another smile to bother her internal thermostat.

'I imagine doctors like your father had it tougher,' Connor said. 'I met an old fellow who was a doctor here forty years ago. He talked about the operations he'd performed on patients he knew were too ill to send to a better facility. I think doctors were expected to have more general skills. I mean, what countrywoman ever went to a specialist to have a baby? Their choice was the local doctor, or the midwife if he happened to be busy.'

'Most of the women where my father practised preferred the midwife,' Caitlin told him.

'Maidenly modesty or because your father treated them too roughly?' Nellie asked, joining them at the table and urging them both to eat with a commanding wave of her hand.

'Actually, it was sentiment. My father was a sentimental man and, no matter how many births he witnessed, he was always moved—usually to tears. Most women, having just given birth, freak out if they see the doctor crying. They assume there's something terribly wrong with their baby. Apparently, knowing his tendency to tears didn't make it any easier for them, so the hospital staff kept him right away from the maternity suite and let him have his little cry in the nursery later.'

Nellie laughed and Connor chuckled.

'I don't believe a word of it,' he said.

'It's the gospel truth,' Caitlin protested, tackling her dinner with a healthy appetite. 'He left Coonebar five years ago, buying into a practice on the coast and cutting back on his workload, but I bet they're still talking about it out there.'

'We had a doctor here once used to sing all the time.' Nellie joined in. 'That drove the women mad as well. Why should he be so happy while we're going through this agony? they'd say. Typical male, that's what he was. The nurses used to try to hush him up, and he'd be quiet for a while, then start up again. Used to do it on the wards, and in Theatre—everywhere.'

'Do you sing?' Caitlin asked, turning to Connor.

'Only in the bath,' he replied.

Four small and trivial words, but there was a smile in his eyes as he said them—and perhaps a challenge. Whatever it was, it teased along Caitlin's nerves and caused tremors low down in her abdomen.

What *was* this weird stuff happening in her usually unsusceptible body?

She concentrated on her meal, hoping her inner reactions weren't apparent to her companions.

Nellie was talking about another doctor now, a young man who'd never been out of the city.

'We had a matron back then who ran the place like a military camp, barking orders right and left, bowing to no one. Poor lad thought he'd be the boss, but Matron soon put him right. Then he asked one of the nurses to have dinner at his house, and she really hit the roof. Gave him a lecture on propriety and what ''good'' girls her nurses were, and threatened him with castration if he didn't toe the line. Or so the story goes.'

'Apart from asking a nurse over to my quarters, which I never did, that could have been me when I arrived. It's hard to know where you fit into the routine when you're a newcomer,' Connor countered when they'd finished laughing at the story.

'Oh, you were never that green,' Nellie protested. 'And Mike was here to back you up and see you didn't do too much wrong. I think men support each other in a work environment.'

Caitlin felt the atmosphere change—as if a door had opened somewhere and a cold breeze had blown through.

Nellie was lifting Connor's empty plate and offering sweets, as placid and unperturbed as ever. So the shift had come from Connor. Caitlin finished her meal and stood up to take her plate across to the washing-up bench. It gave her an excuse to walk past him, to study his face for a moment. No longer smiling—in fact, shut tight, as if laughter was a memory too far away to recall.

'Was Mike here when Dr Robinson started?' he asked.

It was a casual question, one that wouldn't have meant anything if she hadn't felt the coolness in the air and seen the stiffness of his lips as he'd formed the words.

'Angie Robinson?' Nellie screwed up her face as if re-membering such a detail required tremendous concentra-tion. 'Not at first. I think Matron Hobbs was still in charge when Angie came, then Mike arrived a few months later, if I remember it right.'

'Was Matron Hobbs your martinet?'

Nellie seemed puzzled by Connor's question.

'The tough one who threatened the young doctor?' Caitlin explained.

'Oh, no, she'd been gone for ten years by the time Dr Robinson arrived. Matron Hobbs was lovely. You'd know her, Connor, she married that fellow who runs the golf club—never can remember her married name. She'd al-ready given notice and the board had advertised the po-sition but she had a few months to work before the wed-ding.'

From a discreet distance, over by the bench, Caitlin watched Connor's reaction. He was more than interested.

'Did you know Dr Robinson?' The question was out before she could prevent its escape, but the expression that crossed his face made her wish it unsaid. He looked stricken! That was the only word for it. And now Nellie was studying him more closely, although she answered Caitlin when she spoke.

'He's never mentioned it,' she said, setting down a bowl of fruit salad and ice cream in front of Connor as she answered for him. 'And, heaven knows, we've talked about the poor girl often enough. A lovely lass, she was. Quiet, but that's because she was dedicated to the job. All she'd ever wanted to be was a country doctor, she told me, and she worked real hard at it.'

'And are you saying I don't, Nellie?' Connor asked, his voice slightly strained as if speaking was an effort. 'Or that I'm not dedicated because I'm loud and noisy?'

'Get on with you, Connor,' Nellie chided. 'Don't start that teasing talk with me. You know I get all tangled up, and you also know I think you're a good doctor. Would I be wasting my cooking on someone who wasn't?'

'You're letting Caitlin eat in here,' he protested. 'And you've got no idea how good she is at doctoring.'

Nellie chuckled and the comfortable rumble of sound seemed to restore the sense of camaraderie in the room, as if something off-centre had been tilted back into place again.

'She's a different kind of doctor,' Nellie pointed out. 'One of those thinking ones, not doing ones.'

Not thinking too well tonight, Caitlin added silently. She left the bench and crossed back to the table, refusing dessert but pouring herself a cup of coffee from the insulated pot Nellie had set in front of them.

'Want one?' she asked Connor.

He didn't reply but pushed a cup towards her and she filled that one as well, then pushed it back.

He hadn't answered the other question either.

'Why don't you take Caitlin for a walk up to the lookout?' Nellie asked as Connor pushed his bowl away, sighing like a man who'd eaten well. 'Nice night, moon not far past full.'

Caitlin was so surprised by the suggestion she said nothing, but Connor might have been expecting it for all the reaction he showed.

'Matchmaking, Nellie?' he asked in his usual calm way.

'Not at all, just suggesting a bit of exercise for the pair of you. The moon out means you'll be able to see, you dunderhead. Besides, why would I consider matchmaking for the likes of you? There's any number of attractive healthy young women in this town who've done their own trying, to no avail. No, I know when a man's not interested, and I'm sure Caitlin's got enough sense to know it, too.'

Connor smiled at Nellie, then he rose to his feet and turned to Caitlin.

'Well, seeing the moon's bright enough for us to find our way, would you like to walk up to the lookout with me?'

She hesitated. Nellie's words had started so many questions leaping in her mind. She asked the least important.

'There's a lookout within walking distance? I know there are hills out where Mike and Sue live, but the town itself is as level as a pool table, isn't it?'

Connor's smile became warmer, and his eyes lost the blank look they'd had since she'd asked about Angie Robinson.

'Come and see,' he tempted her. 'Let me show you the wonder of Turalla by night.'

She said goodnight to Nellie and walked out of the kitchen with him. For all Nellie's judgement of her 'sense', her heart was behaving as if she had none at all, as if a walk in the moonlight with Connor was a particularly special treat. It hippity-hopped about in her chest, causing breathing difficulties again, and she was so busy trying to settle it down she missed the beginning of his conversation.

'Rid of this coat and get a jacket. Will you need something warm?'

Need something warm? With him walking down the steps beside her, she could feel both his warmth and her own—not to mention the inner heat that coiled low down in her stomach.

'No, thanks,' she said, marvelling at how well her voice was working.

She walked with him across the parking area, through the park where the swings hung motionless.

'I'll wait for you here,' she suggested, and he laughed.

'I've been wondering how long it would be before you gave in to your urge for a swing. Enjoy!'

He touched her lightly on the shoulder, steering her towards the playground.

'I'll be back in a few minutes,' he added.

She settled on the swing, feeling the hardness of the wooden seat beneath her and the familiar feel of the chains in her hands. She pushed herself back as far as she could, then let her body fly forward, lifting her legs to give upward impetus, then lowering them as she swung backwards.

The movements were mechanical, remembered co-ordination of muscles, allowing her mind to go back to Nellie's words and to the question Connor hadn't answered.

Did one thing explain the other? Had he known Angie Robinson? Well enough for her death to have hurt him? Enough for him to lose interest in other women?

For a period of mourning, perhaps?

Or for ever?

No, not for ever, she told herself as the air rushed past and the pure joy of almost flying renewed her confidence in her judgement. She was certain—well, almost certain, not being too practised in the attraction stakes herself—

that he felt some of the attraction she was experiencing. Surely something so strong couldn't be one-sided.

'Isn't there a song about flying to the moon?'

She caught sight of Connor as her body plummeted downwards again. He was leaning against one of the supports of the swing, his jacket slung across one shoulder. His smile made her feel dizzy—although that could have been the swing.

She slowed and stopped, plunging her feet into the soft sand to brake the forward motion.

'I'd like the flying part, but I think the earth holds enough excitement for me,' she said, crossing to where he stood. Particularly at the moment, she could have added as she took in his strong, clean features and saw the sparkle in his eyes.

Is this how love feels? she wondered, and was momentarily stunned by the thought.

Love?

Where did love come into it?

'Well, shall we go?' he asked, and she nodded, too shocked by the path her mind was taking to find the words she needed for a reply.

I must be mad to have gone along with Nellie's ridiculous suggestion, Connor decided as he led Caitlin across the park and up the street towards the silos.

My body behaves badly enough sitting talking to the woman in a brightly lit kitchen, now I've got her on her own with a bit of moonlight thrown in. He lengthened his strides, turning right along the track to the water-tower without turning to see if she was following.

'Is it a race? Did we have a bet about who'd get there first?'

Caitlin's voice made him spin around—and realise his pace must have quickened with his thoughts.

'I'm sorry,' he muttered, as the wretched moonlight made her skin seem luminous, her eyes dark pools of mystery. 'I often walk this way at night, but I'm usually on my own.'

'If you'd prefer to be on your own...' She smiled, but it wasn't a real smile—more a politeness. Damn it, now he'd hurt her with his senseless comment.

'No, no, not at all!'

What was wrong with him? Saying things he didn't mean, stumbling over words.

'I'm sorry,' he said softly, and he lifted his hand and traced the silvered profile with one finger. 'I think you've knocked me senseless.'

Her eyes widened and a faint frown appeared between her eyebrows. His finger touched the tiny crease, smoothing at it as if to erase it.

'I'm sorry, I shouldn't have blurted that out but it seems to be the truth. And I don't know why you're looking puzzled. You're a beautiful woman, you must know the effect you have on men.'

'Not all men,' she said gravely. 'Not on men like you.'

'Men like me?' he echoed.

Something in his voice must have amused her for she smiled, and said, 'Men who seem to have their lives in order, their future mapped out neatly. You know your place in the world and are secure in it. You don't need a woman to hang on your arm like a trophy proclaiming your manhood.'

He shook his head.

'Surely that's not how men see you?'

'Some men,' she said, in the same tone of voice he'd have said 'dog turd'. But then she smiled, a teasing mischievous kind of smile, and added lightly, 'Not men who'd walk a girl up to the lookout on a moonlit night.'

His heart did a kind of convoluted somersault and his lungs stopped working altogether. Unable to form words, he took her hand and led her along the path, relishing the warmth of her fingers, the faint fragrance of night-flowering plants and the silvery moonlight that lit their way.

Somewhere deep inside him, a prissy voice was preaching caution, reminding him there'd been no serious woman in his life since Angie, and it was the beautiful packaging of this one that had floored him, but he ignored it, indulging his emotional self, allowing it a little free rein.

Caitlin liked the feel of her hand in his. It felt right somehow, giving her the same feeling of security she'd had as a child, holding onto her mother's hand. Although that wasn't an analogy Connor would appreciate.

She smiled to herself and quelled an urge to give a little skip and hop of happiness. So he was attracted to her as well—assuming knocking someone senseless indicated some level of attraction. Where to next?

'An affair?'

'I beg your pardon?'

She stopped so suddenly her hand lost his as he turned to face her—obviously stunned by the thought she hadn't meant to say out loud.

'Nothing—just a straying echo of my thoughts that escaped into the air. OK, so I do talk to myself a lot—even when my computer isn't around to listen.'

If she got any hotter, she'd self-combust. She looked into Connor's face, silently pleading with him to drop the subject.

And thought she'd won, for he smiled at her, a singularly sweet smile that triggered a weakness in her bones.

'My thoughts were straying along much the same lines but perhaps we should start with a little "getting to know you" kind of stuff. Say a kiss?'

He waited, as if expecting her to argue or move away, but she could no more have moved than she could have flown to the moon—swing or no swing—so as he bent his head towards her, her lips parted, meeting his with willingness at first, then with pressure as she tried to find something of the man beneath his skin through this silent joining of lips to lips.

As kisses went, it rated badly in the comfort stakes, standing toe to toe on a rocky, slightly sloping path. But it made up for the awkwardness in the fire it lit inside her, the molten flow of energy and desire that now raced through her bloodstream.

She leaned into him, learning the contours of his body as they imprinted themselves on hers, and breathed deeply to replenish the air in her lungs.

'We won't make it to the top if this continues,' he murmured, his fingers playing with her hair, lifting strands of it, then smoothing them back down.

'Do we need to?' she asked. The way she felt at the moment she'd be content to remain right here in his arms for ever.

'What if Nellie asks you about the view?' He hugged her close as if physically agreeing with her unspoken thoughts.

'You could describe it to me.'

She felt the muscles in his chest move as he chuckled, but then he stepped away from her, leaving only cool air where his hard, warm body had been.

'Best we do it properly,' he said, taking her hand once more and leading her along the path. 'Best for many reasons.'

Which it was, she told herself. She barely knew the man and what she did know of him wasn't all that promising. He was too changeable—flaring up at unexpected moments—and secretive—take the Dr Robinson business for a start.

OK, so he's got an attractive face and a great body and his hormones and yours seem to be in sync, but is that enough reason to plunge into an affair? Of course not!

'Talked yourself out of it yet?' he asked.

Add mind-reader—a highly dangerous trait—to the list.

'Out of what?' she demanded, realising, as the path

widened, that they must be close to the top of the small hill.

'Out of the affair,' he said, turning to face her as if to read any attempted evasion in her eyes. 'Don't tell me you haven't spent the last five minutes listing all the reasons why you and I shouldn't get involved. We barely know each other, we're ships passing in the night, hospital gossip, et cetera.'

She grinned at him, and admitted, 'I had the et cetera but hadn't included any of the others on my list. Was that all of yours?'

He sighed.

'Not half of it, lovely lady. Believe me, in another time, another place, I'd whip you off to bed and ravish you so completely we wouldn't surface for a month.' Connor kissed her gently on the lips then lifted his head to add, 'Or let you ravish me. I don't think you'd object, would you, to a little mutual lust and loving?'

He was being honest with her—stressing the physical nature of the attraction—and she liked him more for that forthright approach.

'I'd be on for it,' she admitted, 'although I'm slightly shocked to hear myself saying that. I know women are supposed to be liberated enough to admit their sexual needs and desires, but it's not something that's come up all that often in my life.'

The words stumbled off Caitlin's lips, the heat of embarrassment, not desire, now squirming in her intestines.

'No?' he said softly, letting the breath of the word brush against her lips before his own claimed them once again. The heat swapped sides once more as her body responded with an intensity which must have told him more than words could ever have conveyed.

Surely kissing shouldn't have the power to separate mind and body, to make her ache with longing while her mind sought words to describe the sensations? For a moment she struggled, then she gave in to the purely physical rush, wondering if drug addicts felt like this when they talked about a high.

It was her last thought for a long time, until a discreet cough made them break apart. Caitlin eased her body away from Connor's and turned towards the view as a man walking his dog appeared on the path.

Was the moonlight bright enough to show the flaring heat of embarrassment she'd felt flow to her face? She looked up, pretending an interest in the stars, seeking a formation she might recognise, anything to distract her from this moment.

'Evening, Connor,' the stranger said, lifting his hand in a salute. 'Lovely night.'

'Beautiful,' Connor agreed. He kept one arm clamped around Caitlin's shoulders to try to still the trembling in her body.

Or was it in his, conveyed to hers along his leaping nerves and into her skin and bones and flesh?

No, better he didn't think about her flesh.

He watched Ron Andrews walk his dog around the top of the hill, as if the circumnavigation was a ritual they couldn't miss, then waved again when Ron called goodnight and headed down the path.

'He's not a gossip,' he said to Caitlin when Ron and the dog had been swallowed up by the shadows.

She stopped peering at the sky as if continued study of it might reveal to her the secrets of the universe and turned to look at him as she spoke.

'I think gossip would be more harmful to you than me, Connor.'

The lovely cadence of her voice washed over him, while her eyes expressed concern. How long had it been since someone had shown concern for him? Apart from Nellie—and maybe Sue Nelson?

Since Angie?

After the break with her, he'd turned to work, determined to succeed if only to prove to himself that he'd made the right choice. He hadn't actually avoided women, but he hadn't sought them out or welcomed their attentions—concerned or otherwise.

Now this beautiful woman was looking at him as if she cared what happened to him.

'Dangerous stuff,' he muttered, and saw her eyebrows rise.

'Gossip? Has it affected you before?'

He smiled, then gave a soft chuckle.

'I was thinking of concern, not gossip,' he explained. 'But to answer your question, no, I'm gossip-free, both here in Turalla and in my blameless past.'

'And you intend to keep it that way?'

She spoke lightly but he knew there was an underlying intent behind the words.

'Not if it means you and I can't pursue a friendship— maybe even a courtship.' He looked into her eyes, willing her to believe him. 'OK, so we can't let our hormones run wild, not right here and now, but surely we can spend some free time together, to discover where this attraction might lead. Is it just a physical magnetism, or might something more lie beyond our rampant libidos? Are you game to find out, Caitlin O'Shea?'

She smiled at him and his heart told him it wasn't physical—well, not entirely. Just because his body reacted to every expression on her face, every tonal change of her voice, that didn't mean...

What?

Perhaps he was better not thinking about this at all. Just act and react.

'I'm game,' she said, and this time she kissed him, reaching up to brush her mouth across his, then sliding her hands around his neck, drawing him closer, deepening the kiss until he felt he was drowning in a sea of desire.

Act and react? Bad move! Hell, the reaction was so strong it hurt...

'You'd better have a look at the view,' he muttered,

moving away from her and waving his hand towards the lights of the town. 'It's actually better from Mike's place.'

'Having second thoughts?' she asked, following him to where he clung to the railing of the viewing platform.

'About what?' He tried to remember the conversation they'd been having before the reaction. Something about libidos? That might explain…

'I'm sorry, I lost it just then.' Connor turned and touched her cheek, then felt the silky strands of her hair. An image of it spread out across his pillow did little for his self-control. 'I asked if you were game, didn't I? If we should see where this attraction leads?'

She looked at him, not smiling, but there was a sparkle in her eyes when she spoke, the kind of sparkle that made him think of starlight.

'Do you always forget the question before you've been given the answer?'

He touched his finger to her lips, testing to see if they were simply skin with flesh beneath them or some more potent form of tissue that drove thoughts from the minds of men.

'I heard the answer,' he told her gravely. 'You said, ''I'm game.'' That's when I lost it.'

She took his hand and held it, effectively stopping his exploration of her lips. But only because she needed them for something else, he realised as once again she stood on tiptoe, repeated the words 'I'm game' so he could feel as well as hear them, then she pressed her mouth to his and his body swooped out of control once again.

'As long as it doesn't interfere with my work,' she added, when they finally moved apart and began to walk towards the path.

'Heaven forbid!' he muttered. This was hardly the moment to tell her she'd been interfering with his work, getting tied up in all his thought processes, since he'd first set eyes on her. 'So how's it going?' he asked, aiming at some kind of normal conversation.

'What going?' she asked, then she laughed as if her own thoughts were as tangled as his. 'My work? OK.'

'That's very noncommittal.' He was making conversation, nothing more, yet his comment must have rubbed against her in some way for she stopped and spun to face him.

'I don't believe you care one way or another about my work,' she said, in a very different voice to the one that had talked of their mutual attraction. That voice had been warm and husky—not cool and challenging.

'I do and don't,' he muttered, knowing he'd lost ground he might never recover. 'It bothers me and I'm not going to pretend it doesn't, but I can't deny the premise of it, and I can't ignore the fact that Turalla does present a unique opportunity for science to look more closely at genetic links.'

'But the town's not bothered, Connor,' she argued, her lovely eyes pleading for his support. 'At least not the people of the town I've spoken to. I'm not only talking about the parents of the children, but other citizens in shops, around the hospital—Nellie and Melissa, even Mike and Sue. They're not unhappy, so why are you?'

That's asking you, old son!

He shrugged and grimaced and knew Caitlin wasn't going to accept a body movement or a facial expression as an answer. Could he use a presentiment of fear as a rational argument? Not likely! Certainly not with Miss Scientific Researcher here.

'I don't know,' he said. That was partly the truth because he didn't know why the fear still lingered. 'But I am—and all I can do is ask you to tread warily. What people say directly to you, how they act when you are present, it isn't always the whole story.'

'You mean Granny Russell could be plotting my demise even as we speak?' She was teasing him, her lips curling into a smile, her eyes sparkling with delight.

He tried to respond, to return her smile, but coldness

had spread out from his heart, pumping through his veins where heat had flowed a little earlier.

Damn the woman! Why couldn't she be here to write a book on country hospitals or to study the impact of isolation on unmarried country doctors? The mating habits of koalas might be good! Anything but the leukaemia cluster.

'I wouldn't be surprised,' he said lightly. 'She's a woman of great common sense and probably recognises a witch when she sees one.'

He kissed her then because he didn't want to talk about his fear and doubted he could conceal it completely from her probing mind and questioning eyes.

Eventually, they walked again, retracing their steps, arm in arm, drawing warmth and human comfort from each other, hiding the differences that could be barriers to this togetherness. But when they reached the end of the path, she drew apart so they headed back towards the hospital as friends, not would-be lovers.

'The golf club serves dinner on Friday and Saturday evenings. I usually eat up there with Sue and Mike on Saturdays. Would you like to come—to join us?' Connor asked the question as they neared the hospital entrance, reluctant to part from her until he knew for certain when he'd see her again.

'Didn't Sue say you hosted a barbecue on Sundays? Social outings on both Saturday and Sunday? What a hectic life you country people lead.'

'The Sunday thing's become a tradition but, while it's held at my place, it's more a joint effort. Everyone brings their own meat and most of the women bring a bowl of salad. They must have some kind of system because we never end up with fourteen bowls of lettuce and none of tomato.'

'A nice tradition,' she replied. 'Is it only hospital staff?'

'Mostly, although they all bring their husbands, wives or kids, so we get a real mix. The kids play in the park, the women chat and the men stand around the barbecue, prod the meat and tell lies to each other.'

Caitlin laughed at that, the soft husky sound that thrilled along his nerves. Then the laughter stopped. Suddenly? Or did it only seem that way?

'I'll expect you to come—everyone will—but we're talking Saturday, not Sunday at the moment. Dinner tomorrow night?'

She didn't reply immediately but stared ahead as if some movement in the hospital had caught her eye.

'I'd like that,' she said, but her voice had lost its carefree tone and she was frowning as if uncertain. Of what she'd seen, or about having dinner with him?

'Oh, it's Anne,' she murmured, almost to herself, as Anne Jackson appeared on a lighted part of the veranda.

'Did you think you'd seen a ghost?' he asked, wanting to see her smile again.

'Something like that,' she muttered with an undertone of something that sounded very like fear.

But he was the fearful one! He the one whose instinct was urging him to send her far away.

He walked her around to the house, as nervous as a teenager on a first date. Would she ask him in? Should he accept? The sensors picked them up, flooding the area with light. The moment was coming closer and he was twitchy with anticipation! Then she put her hand on the doorknob, turned it and pushed the door open, and his ridiculous adolescent thoughts were swept away by anger.

'You didn't lock the door?' he demanded, his voice almost shaking with emotion.

She turned towards him, obviously stunned by his attack.

'But I did lock it, Connor,' she whispered, her brown eyes huge in her pale face.

She reached into her pocket and pulled out the heavy, old-fashioned key.

CHAPTER EIGHT

CONNOR stepped in front of Caitlin, snapping on the light, looking around the room.

'Stay there while I check the other rooms,' he ordered, but fear for him made Caitlin follow. Surely, if someone was inside, two of them would stand more chance.

Not that there was much to check. One long stride took him down the hall, peering into the bathroom on one side, then her bedroom on the other.

Caitlin caught up with him as he pushed open the bedroom door, then turned back, arms outstretched to ward her off.

But one glimpse was enough to see the devastation—a great gash like a black wound in the screen of her computer and thick shards of the shattered screen scattered across the bed.

Connor's arms closed around her as the involuntary cry escaped her lips, and he held her close for a moment then moved her purposefully back into the living room.

'I'm phoning Ned Withers, he's the police sergeant,' he announced, as he all but pushed her down in a chair. 'Then I'm going to pack up your things and shift you over to my place.'

Caitlin didn't argue. She was shaking too much for her lips to form words, while her mind seemed to have shut down, numbed by the violence of the attack on her computer. Then, as the numbness thawed, the questions surfaced.

'Why?' she asked Connor. 'How can my research upset someone to this degree? I'm not looking into family secrets, or trying to uncover illegal activity. We're talking about children here, and the possibility of saving children's lives!'

He'd finished his phone call and come to sit on the arm of the chair, slipping one arm around her shoulders.

'I don't know, Caitlin, but someone does resent your presence. I don't suppose I can persuade you to leave town until that someone's caught?'

She looked up at him and saw the deep concern she heard in the roughness of his voice reflected in his eyes.

'No,' she told him, straightening her shoulders. 'And what's more, I'm not leaving this house—scurrying over to your place like a frightened mouse. Whoever did this is a coward—leaving notes and smashing a computer.'

'Leaving notes? What do you mean? You've had a threatening note?'

Connor had leapt back to his feet and now loomed angrily over her.

'And you didn't think to mention this to Mike or me? Good grief, Caitlin, it's not as if you're not an intelligent woman! You must know people who leave threatening notes aren't right in the head, yet you did nothing about it.'

Caitlin glared right back at him.

'I did do something about it. I screwed it up and threw it away. And it wasn't a threatening letter, just a page out of a children's fairy-tale book.'

Connor looked at her as if she was mad, but no way was she going to add any further explanation.

Fortunately, at that moment the lights went on again outside and a car pulled up. Connor walked to the door, opening it to admit a large man in uniform.

'Ned, this is Caitlin O'Shea, a doctor doing some research here in Turalla. We had dinner with Nellie at the hospital then walked up to the lookout. Came back to find the door unlocked and this.'

He led Ned, who'd shaken hands with Caitlin during the introduction, into the bedroom.

'Blimey!' Ned said, crunching his way over shattered plastic to inspect the machine.

'Best I take it with me,' he said, then he looked around.

'Anything else out of place, Doctor?'

Caitlin, who'd followed the two men, looked helplessly around. Her first view of the damaged computer had shown her the shattered screen, but now she looked again she realised whoever had done it had delivered not one blow but many, hitting at the silvery box over and over again, and with force enough to bend, buckle and in places shatter the outer case.

She put a hand over her mouth as nausea roiled in her stomach and headed for the bathroom, where she perched on the side of the bath until the sick feeling subsided.

Connor found her there some time later.

'Come on,' he said, his tone brusque, the would-be lover of earlier this evening gone. 'I've packed your things.'

Caitlin stared at him, but her mind, already battling to accept the damage someone had inflicted on her computer, couldn't make sense of the change.

'I'll go to a motel,' she told him.

'No, you won't. You'll come to my place. I told Ned that's where you'll be if he needs to speak to you. The choice is there, or Mike and Sue's, and I know from my baby-sitting experience there that those kids wake with the dawn and the sofa bed is terrible.'

He took her arm and eased her to her feet, then moved away, picking up her suitcase and heading purposefully towards the door. Left with little option but to follow, Caitlin went after him, then remembered her laptop, tucked away under the bed.

'Wait,' she called to Connor, who either didn't hear her or decided to ignore her. But she wasn't going without it. Not anywhere. And possibly never again.

In the bedroom, Ned was dusting what she assumed was fingerprint powder over the table. Treading carefully, and keeping well out of his way, Caitlin worked her way to the side of the bed then knelt and reached underneath.

Her heart was thudding with apprehension as she felt under the mattress base, fingers seeking the slim outline of the laptop. Her relief when she finally made contact was so great she almost sobbed with joy.

She drew it out and clutched it to her chest, strangely reassured although she knew she had back-up for the work she'd done both on CD and on the computer back at the lab.

'Oh!'

Connor must have returned to look for her, and met her in the doorway.

'So you haven't lost all your work?'

It was a question, but the tone of it was strange, as if he knew he should be feeling happy for her, but wasn't.

'I'm not totally stupid!' she snapped, 'and in case you're wondering, this isn't the only back-up I have. All the information I've gathered has gone to the lab in Brisbane as well, so all someone destroyed was an inanimate object.'

'Someone *violently* destroyed,' Connor amended, his words as cold and hard as chips of ice.

Caitlin shivered, perturbed as much by the change in Connor as the coldness in his voice.

'Ned's parked behind your car. Do you mind walking across?'

She wanted to protest again but knew he wouldn't listen, the warm, sensitive man who'd urged her to have a swing replaced by this emotionless authoritarian. So she nodded glumly and trudged behind him, past the hospital kitchen, where they'd laughed with Nellie, and the park and swing, where she'd flown so high and joyfully just a few hours earlier.

'I'll put you in my room,' Connor announced as he led the way up the steps and into the kitchen.

'And sleep across the doorway?' Caitlin snapped at

him. 'Don't be silly, Connor. If the person wanted to harm me, there's been plenty of opportunity while I slept at the house. I'll use your spare bedroom—the one I used the day I arrived.'

He turned and scowled at her.

'You'll sleep in my room and, no, I won't sleep across the door. I'll sleep beside you.'

'Beside me? In bed with me?'

His face lightened for a moment and he almost smiled.

'An hour ago it wasn't such a horrific idea,' he reminded her. 'But this will be purely platonic. I'll even sleep on top of the sheet if you like.'

He'd dropped her case on the floor, and now he turned and walked across to the bench beneath the window. He put his hands on it and leaned forward, shoulders bowed as he stared out into the dark night.

'You asked earlier if I knew Angie,' he said, his voice little more than a harsh whisper. 'The answer's yes, Caitlin. I knew Angie. At one stage we were engaged. But she wanted to work in the outback and I didn't want to leave the career I was carving out for myself in the city. We broke up and she came out here.'

Caitlin wasn't sure how she felt—too many emotions chasing each other through her body. Then a flash of understanding and one emotion surfaced, pity beating off jealousy, astonishment and confusion. Pity for Connor who carried guilt that he'd let the woman he loved go alone to the country where she'd died a terrible death.

She stepped forward and put her arms around him, resting her body against his back.

'Do you really think things might have been different if you'd been here as well?' she asked him.

'We wouldn't have been here,' he said, turning and linking his arms loosely around her body. 'We'd have gone to a bigger town—one that needed two doctors. Turalla could do with one and a half, but the logistics of getting doctors to practise in rural areas are such that the department will only ever appoint one.'

He spoke without emotion and Caitlin felt his hold was less an embrace than somewhere to put his arms. She took a deep breath, then asked the question that had to be asked.

'And how does you not going to the country with Angie lead to us sharing a bed tonight?'

He looked down into her eyes, his own dark with what she guessed were memories and regrets.

'I've no reason for it, and I've no proof, though, believe me, I've looked for it, but I can't believe Angie's death was an accident.'

The words seemed to hang in the air between them, invoking a superstitious fear that made Caitlin shiver.

She stepped away from Connor, who didn't try to hold her, and rubbed her arms.

'So, tonight we share my bed and tomorrow you leave town,' he said, picking up her case and carrying it into the bedroom.

Caitlin shook her head, unable to believe this new edict.

'Like hell I will!' she yelled, storming after him. 'Neither will I share your bed. Give me that case. I'm sleeping in the spare room. If it makes you happier I'll shut the doors and push something against them. Then tomorrow I'll move into a motel which, I'm sure, will be modern enough to have doors with deadbolts and safety chains as well.'

She grabbed her case out of his hand and stomped back through the kitchen and laundry to the veranda and the spare bedroom where she'd slept not so very long ago.

She must have been mad to let her emotions run amok with Connor Clarke. The man was so screwed up! So riddled with guilt and remorse and bitterness he was seeing danger where none existed.

Well, maybe some, but danger to things, not people…

She had opened her case and was digging through it for her nightshirt while mentally berating herself.

Found it and threw it on the bed, then dug again, this time for her toiletries.

Fruitless effort…

They'd been in the bathroom—where she'd been while Connor had packed. And doubtless they were still there.

Well, she wasn't going back there tonight, or asking Connor to go, so she'd rub some of his toothpaste around her teeth with her finger and get the rest of her gear to-morrow.

On her way to the motel.

Footsteps sounded on the veranda then Connor tapped on her door.

'Would you like a cup of tea or some other kind of drink before you go to bed?'

'The polite host offering succour to the unwelcome guest,' Caitlin sniped, and saw his tall, rangy figure flinch slightly, but then he straightened.

'I'll take that as a no, shall I?' he said, ultra-cool.

Caitlin nodded. The emotional strain of the evening had combined with her regret for the distance that now stretched between them and formed a lump in her throat.

She turned away so he wouldn't see her trying to swal-low it and hold back the foolish tears gathering in her eyes.

'OK,' he said, and she heard the footsteps retreat.

Slumping down on the bed, she buried her head in her pillow, but instead of crying, she pummelled it, releasing some of the tension that had her insides twisted into knots.

She must have fallen asleep, waking to darkness—had Connor come to check on her again and turned off the light? Her dress was crumpled and her mouth felt like the inside of a parrot's cage, so she clambered wearily to her feet, stretched, then fumbled along the wall, seeking the light switch. Found it, and turned it on. She'd need the light it shed out onto the veranda to make her way to the bathroom.

It was too late to be splashing around under a shower, but she'd have a good wash and change into her night-shirt. She grabbed it and headed out, only realising she wasn't alone on the veranda when a small sound, more like a snort than a snore, alerted her to another presence.

Connor wasn't asleep across her doorway. Oh, no, he'd put his swag at least a couple of metres from it, but placed so anyone creeping around on the veranda would be sure to trip over him.

Caitlin held back the urge to kick him, instead creeping past, then once in the bathroom she realised the possibil-ities for revenge his action had provided for her. She'd sleep in his bed after all. Let him spend an uncomfortable night in his swag on the veranda, then realise in the morn-ing how futile he'd been as a sentry.

She'd just decided this would serve him right when she remembered what had passed between them earlier. Remembered all she knew of him, and accepted that his behaviour stemmed only from an urge to protect her.

She might not want or need his protection, but he didn't deserve that she make light of it. She crept quietly back the way she'd come.

Connor was gone when she woke again—gone from the veranda and the house, if the silence echoing through it was any indication.

Caitlin dressed, then walked into the kitchen, wishing Connor was there so they could talk properly again, with-out all the angst and emotion of the previous evening.

'Hi, sleepyhead!'

It was Melissa who greeted her, coming in from the veranda, a magazine dangling from the fingers of her right hand.

'Connor asked me to see you got some breakfast. He told me what happened—that's terrible.'

Melissa was so genuinely sympathetic, Caitlin knew she'd be an ally.

'Who am I upsetting in this town?' she asked. 'Who would do something like this, and why?'

Melissa obviously took the questions seriously, for she frowned as she filled the kettle and turned it on.

'I honestly don't know,' she said, shaking her head to emphasise this point. 'I can't see how what you're doing could hurt anyone, and yet surely only someone who was hurt, or feared being hurt, could do such a thing.'

'Hurt!' Caitlin echoed the word Melissa had used. 'Hurt how? I know you don't mean physically, but no one can ever be blamed for causing cancer, so finding out more wouldn't hurt them that way. Reputation? That can be damaged, but not by what I'm doing.'

'Relationships could be hurt,' Melissa suggested. 'Do you want toast? Or there's cereal. Connor said he knew you ate cereal.'

'Toast, thanks,' Caitlin responded, then switched back to Melissa's suggestion. 'Relationships?' she echoed. 'But if the women I've interviewed feared that what I'm doing could harm their relationship with their husbands, surely they wouldn't have talked to me.'

Melissa shrugged.

'Maybe it isn't the talking to them but what they think you might do next. Angie was taking blood samples from the families who had a child with leukaemia. You know, cousins and things. Maybe they think you'll do that next.'

Melissa spoke casually, but the statement filled Caitlin with confusion.

'Why was Angie taking blood? And if you think what happened to her was an accident, why mention it?'

Melissa appeared to be startled by Caitlin's vehemence, for she turned, kettle in hand, frowning at the questions.

'I think she was taking blood to check no one else in the family was affected. Isn't what you're doing completely different?'

Melissa ignored the 'accident' question, but Caitlin guessed that wasn't deliberate. She'd wanted to clarify the first point first.

'It is,' Caitlin agreed. 'That's if the specimens she took *were* for testing for leukaemia, not for some other reason. I'd hate to think I'm wasting my time following a line someone else has already followed to a dead end.'

'It was a dead end for Angie,' a deep voice said, and Caitlin turned to find Connor had come quietly up the stairs and was standing in the doorway behind her.

His blunt words had shocked her, but before she could protest he was talking to Melissa, thanking her for waiting—dismissing her, but with kindness and a genuine smile.

He waited until she'd reached the bottom of the steps and turned towards the surgery next door, then he turned back to Caitlin. 'I've phoned your boss—Mike had a home number for him—and he agrees you should return to Brisbane.'

The blue-green eyes were fixed on her, his resolve easy to read, but she hadn't got to where she was without a truckload of resolve herself. She damped down the flare of temper his interference had caused, knowing she had to make her point without histrionics.

'I'm not going, Connor,' she said quietly. 'I'll be careful but I won't leave town.'

He was, at the most, two metres away, yet as she looked at him she felt the great divide that now separated them. 'You said something once before—about me not having had to choose between my career and something else. Or someone else, as it must have been in your case. Well, I'm choosing now, Connor, and if it means, thanks to your phone call, that I'll lose my career, then so be it, but *I am not leaving town.*'

He looked so shocked she almost laughed, but the sick feeling in her stomach assured her there was nothing even vaguely amusing about this situation.

The anger she'd reined in earlier rose again.

Forgetting the breakfast Melissa had begun to fix for her, Caitlin swept out of the kitchen and through to the spare bedroom where she repacked her nightshirt, closed her case and headed back.

Connor was still standing where she'd left him, just inside the back door.

'Excuse me!' Caitlin muttered, not really caring if he moved or not. In fact, she was tempted to let the case swing out so its hard edge caught his knee.

She resisted the temptation and continued on her way, down the steps, across the park, past the swings—moving determinedly towards the little house behind the hospital.

Connor watched her go, worry twisting in his gut, his concern for her so all-encompassing he wanted to yell and rant and rave at her—or at someone.

First, though, he had to get through morning surgery. He was already late and patients would be cramming into the too-small waiting room. And surely nothing would happen to that stubborn, determined woman at nine o'clock on a Saturday morning.

He went to work but, though he tried to put it all out of his mind, images of Caitlin swam before his eyes, while the feel of her was imprinted on every sensory receptor in every millimetre of his skin.

What was worse, he realised as he checked Mrs Rennie's ulcerated leg, now he'd alienated Caitlin he was no longer in a position to provide even minimal protection for her.

'I'm sorry, Mrs Rennie, but it's not getting better. I'd like to admit you to hospital for a few days. I can give you a stronger antibiotic in a drip into your arm and while you're there the nurses can change the dressing more regularly. If that doesn't improve it, we might have to think about a skin graft.'

The elderly woman smiled at him.

'As long as you use someone else's skin,' she told him.

'I don't want you peeling off any of mine. A bit of your own would do.'

He dredged a smile from somewhere, knowing how much she enjoyed a little joke.

'You'd take a bit of peeling, Mrs R.,' he said, helping her to her feet and out the door then giving Margaret, his nurse, instructions for the dressing.

'Melissa, would you phone the hospital and ask them to get a bed ready to admit Mrs Rennie?'

He looked around the waiting room, seeking the patient's daughter, Charlene.

'You're going to put her into hospital?' Charlene, who'd heard his conversation with Melissa, asked.

Connor nodded. 'I can treat it better in there,' he said.

'You might also be able to make sure she stays off her feet and rests the leg the way you've been telling her to. I've tried to make her do it, Connor, but she won't listen to me.'

'Do women ever listen to anyone?' Connor muttered, and Charlene laughed.

'Only when the advice agrees with what they want to do themselves,' she told him, then, as her mother came out of the treatment room, she stepped forward to take her arm and lead her gently back out to the car.

'We've time to go home and pack some things for her?' Charlene turned back to ask Connor.

'Of course,' he said, then he called his next patient.

'He's just not well,' Mary Cousins told Connor, ushering four-year-old Sam towards the consulting room. 'He's tired, doesn't want to play...'

Fear gripped Connor, as strong as a hand around his throat, making it difficult to breathe—to speak.

He helped Sam onto the examination table and stood beside him, talking to him as he touched and prodded him, gently pressing his palm into the child's abdomen, feeling him flinch slightly, then easing the lower eyelid down to check his eyes.

'Is it…?'

Mary couldn't say the word, but Connor knew and shook his head.

'I won't know for certain until we've run a blood test, but it looks more like hepatitis to me. Have you noticed any change to his urine?'

Mary frowned, then shook her head.

'He's at a private age,' she said, but Sam had evidently followed the conversation.

'My wee's real dark,' he said, and Connor smiled.

'I thought it might have been,' he told the child. 'Now, we need to know how you got this bug. Have you been out camping lately?'

Mary was still considering the question when Sam answered again.

'I went camping with Daniel's family a few weeks ago. It was wicked. We went to a place where there were heaps of big lizards walking all around the camping area.'

'Lake Terrimac,' Mary said.

'Did you drink water out of the lake?' Connor asked.

'No, Mr Collins said not to, but the day we went hiking up along the creek, I had a drink out of that.'

'That could be the source of it,' Connor said to Mary. 'People camp right along that creek and they aren't always careful about protecting the environment. If this is hepatitis I'll have the water out there tested and more signs erected warning people not to drink it without boiling it first.'

'So, what do we do about Sam? Are there tablets?'

Connor shook his head.

'Just rest and plenty of fluids. I'll get the test results back in a couple of days. I'll have Melissa phone you if I need to see you again. It's most likely hepatitis A which is the most common form and it shouldn't affect him in any way later on. Hepatitis B is the one you hear more about which has long-term effects.'

He talked a little longer, and when Mary was satisfied

showed her out, the phrase 'long-term effects' echoing in his head.

That's what he feared Caitlin O'Shea had had on him! Described it exactly.

He'd have to think about that situation—try to make amends of some kind—even if only so he could stay at least professionally close to the stubborn wretch while she was here.

His morning continued, busy enough to keep most thoughts of the shapely blonde at bay, though little things, like the phrase, brought her to mind so easily he wondered if he'd ever get her out of his head.

Back at the little house, Caitlin had cleaned up the mess in her bedroom, taking the bed cover outside and shaking the fragments off it. Hardest to remove was the dark powder—she assumed fingerprint powder—which covered the doorknob and was brushed around the lock and the jamb.

Being physically active soothed her anger, and by the time she'd set up her laptop where the PC had been, she was regretting not her decision to stay on in Turalla but the distance it had put between herself and Connor, just when getting closer had seemed such a tiny step away.

She concentrated on her work, seeking connections, transferring her findings back to a large sheet of paper, where she could use different colours to pick out the familial relationships.

Red and green were most predominant—Russells and a family called Wetherby, although they seemed to have more daughters than sons so none of the current generation had the Wetherby surname.

She was thinking about the genetic likelihood of a family producing more daughters than sons when the phone rang.

'Anthea Cummings, Caitlin. I'm sorry it's short notice, but I'm free this morning if you've time to pop out.'

Delighted at the thought of getting away from the town

for a while, Caitlin agreed, checked she had the right directions, then packed up her laptop and papers and headed out of the house.

Locking it seemed pointless now, though she'd have to decide if she was going to stay in the house or move to a motel. If she decided to stay, she should get a better lock—if only to prove to Connor she wasn't as careless as he assumed.

Connor…

Thoughts of him—of the kisses they'd shared—filtered through her head as she drove out of town. They interrupted when she tried to think of work, and muddled her usually tidy mind.

Think Wetherbys and Russells—think family ties and DNA and maybe finding one small clue that will help towards ending just one form of childhood leukaemia for ever.

But Connor kept intruding so she was glad when she finally found the property she was seeking and turned off the main road, bouncing over the grid and down a long tree-lined drive towards the house.

Anthea Cummings had started on a family tree, and was happy for Caitlin to take a copy of it back to the hospital.

'It gives me a framework to hang the relationships on,' Caitlin said, when she'd finished asking questions and was leaving the house.

'I just hope it helps,' Anthea told her. 'So far, nothing else has given us even a hint of what might have caused the cluster. These things happen—that's all the city doctors would say.'

Caitlin smiled at her and shook her head.

'It's all anyone can say, unfortunately, until we know more about the disease and how it's transmitted. I'm trying out a theory based more on why than how. Why one child gets it but another doesn't. Like your family. Lucy's the youngest of four. The older ones are now unlikely candidates, yet all have varying combinations of your genes and your husband's.'

'So why can't you use the sisters and brothers of all affected children for a study, instead of doing all this family history stuff?'

They were standing on the back steps of Anthea's house, looking out over dusty brown acres where cattle grazed, seemingly content with the dry grass nature had provided for them.

'Do you have a breeding programme for your cattle?' Caitlin asked her.

'Of course!' Anthea paused, then nodded. 'Yes, I understand. It's not necessarily just Hal's and my genes that have gone into the kids, it's all our ancestors'. We've a bull here we bred ourselves and his bloodlines go back to Hal's great-grandfather's original herd. They proved their toughness in these harsh lands, so we try to keep some of that blood in the stock, although nowadays emphasis is on rapid growth and a low fat to muscle ratio.'

After a few more minutes of chat, Caitlin said goodbye and left, driving back over one of the low ranges Connor had pointed out the night they'd driven to Mike's place for dinner.

Ironbark and wattle grew in profusion, and eucalypts Caitlin didn't recognise by name. It was here in the timbered country that gold had been found, here that a few miners still eked out a living.

She peered into the trees and saw thick undergrowth. Yes, it would be easy to lose your way in there. But to fall into a mine shaft? Mine shafts usually had mullock heaps around them—piles of unproductive rock thrown out as the miners dug for gold. You'd have to climb up over the heaps of stone and rubble before you could fall down.

Wouldn't you?

Caitlin shook her head, not familiar enough with mines or mine shafts to really know the answer.

Why was Angie Robinson's death niggling in her mind?

Because she'd been a woman and her death had occurred at a time when people had been in town investigating the cancer cluster?

Or because of the damage inflicted on her own computer?

A clearing by the side of the road caught her attention and she slammed on the brakes, juddered to a halt over the rough gravel, then backed up.

A clearing, and on the far side of it a pile of stones. The mullock heap of a mine shaft?

Well, it was close enough to the road for her to investigate. Now was the time to dispel her silly fancies.

She turned off the engine, remembered Melissa's description of Dr Robinson's car and removed the keys from the ignition. Not that anything was likely to happen here. The road might be gravel but she'd passed plenty of traffic on it as she'd driven out to Anthea's.

She crossed the clearing, keeping a wary eye out for snakes. As she drew closer to her objective, she saw the pile of stones was, in fact, a circle, exactly how she'd imagined a mine-shaft mullock heap would look.

Treading carefully, she climbed up, then went no further, for the black hole of the shaft yawned up at her.

Could she slip and fall in there if she moved unwarily?

She remembered Connor talking about snakes in the shafts and shuddered at the thought but, looking around, she wondered if falling accidentally was likely.

In fact, she could probably step, with care, right down to the lip of that hole and peer into it without endangering life or limb. And if she were to lose her footing, surely she'd be able to grab at the edge and haul herself back up, or turn her body as she fell, and go across the hole instead of into it.

'Well!' she muttered to herself. 'That hasn't helped you much, but perhaps other mines are wider and deeper.'

She clambered down to level ground again, another question pounding in her head. Why did you need to look? her brain kept asking. What could you have proved, one way or another?

It would have been nice to know it *could* have been an accident.

The answer came to her as clearly as if someone had spoken it—so precisely, in fact, that she looked around to see if someone had.

'Oh, hell!' she grumbled. 'As if you're not confused enough about Connor, without having Angie Robinson's ghost haunting you as well.'

She hurried back to her car—her speed machine—but drove very slowly home. One doctor dying an accidental death was enough for any country town.

CHAPTER NINE

CONNOR was waiting for her when Caitlin returned, sitting on the back veranda of the hospital where Nellie often sat.

He walked across to the car as she pulled up, opening the door for her and holding it.

She looked up at him, seeing the dark hair, straight nose, lips that could have posed for a Michelangelo sculpture.

Her stomach knotted with desire while her heart did the tachycardia thing again, but it was her mind that was most befuddled, unable to take in his presence, or work out a reason for it.

Unless...

'Have you come to yell at me again? To order me home like some eight-year-old barred from school for disciplinary reasons?'

'I didn't yell at you,' he said, reaching in to take the laptop she'd picked up off the seat beside her.

'You did so!' she argued. 'When the door wasn't locked. You yelled then.'

He was so close she could see the movement of muscles beneath his skin as his lips twitched into a very small and, she guessed, reluctant smile.

'You can't call that a yell,' he told her, but though the smile widened it didn't move into his eyes. This obviously wasn't the end of the war, just a temporary truce. 'If you want a yell, come into theatre when our flying surgeon, David Ogilvie, is there.'

'I've never thought being a surgeon gave a person the right to be rude in any way, let alone yell,' Caitlin said, as Connor straightened, allowing her to breathe almost normally again. She was talking about the flying surgeon but thinking about Connor's behaviour.

Wondering why there was a truce, and if it was genuine or simply a ploy to lull her into a false sense of security so he could attack again from another direction.

After all, this was the man who, only this morning, had gone behind her back to her boss...

'Me neither,' he was saying as he headed, with the laptop, towards the house. He turned to see if she'd got out of the car before adding, 'I've been waiting for you, to let you in. I put a new lock on your door.'

Caitlin restrained herself, with difficulty, from executing a little dance step. Surely putting a new lock on her door meant he'd given in about her staying and they could be friends again.

'Thank you,' she said demurely, and refrained from telling him she'd intended doing it herself.

She even smiled, hoping to tempt him into a proper one this time, but he'd already disappeared inside the house. All she could do was follow, though she felt a diffidence about being with him in that enclosed space, where the differences between them might be too hard to avoid.

But perhaps, now they'd both cooled down, they could discuss these differences like reasonable adults.

She might even be able to get him to see her point...

The loud ringing of the phone forced her to stop dithering, and she walked in to find Connor had put her laptop on the bench, with two new keys beside it, and now looked as if he was on the point of leaving.

'The keys are there,' he said, and departed.

Caitlin snatched up the phone, furious with the caller who'd interrupted at such a critical moment.

It was Sue.

'I wondered if you'd join us for dinner at the golf club tonight,' Sue said, and Caitlin remembered that's what she and Connor had been discussing when they'd discovered the unlocked door.

'Do come,' Sue pressed, taking her silence for doubt. 'I'd love to talk to you again, and I know your time here is limited.'

Had Connor put Sue up to this—knowing that if he'd asked, she wouldn't have gone?

'You are still there?' Sue demanded.

'Yes, I'm here. I was thinking,' Caitlin said.

'It wasn't that hard a question,' Sue teased. 'And the chef up there is fantastic. Young and self-taught but with grand ambitions to go a long way in chefery or whatever it's called.'

'I'd love to come,' Caitlin found herself saying. 'What time, and where's the golf club?'

'I'll get Mike to pick you up. I'm playing so he'll feed the kids and hand them over to the sitter. We can drop you home as well.'

Caitlin thanked Sue and hung up but the bitter taste of disappointment lingered on her lips. She realised she'd been assuming—or at least hoping—Connor would be there, but Sue wouldn't be offering a lift home if that was the case...

She fixed herself a sandwich for lunch, then wondered why she'd bothered. Had anyone ever considered a diet based on a disastrous love life? She'd walked out on breakfast, now couldn't eat her lunch. Not that where she'd reached with Connor could be considered a 'love life'. It had just come closer than anything she'd experienced lately.

'Get real!' she muttered to herself, opening her laptop and setting the notes she'd made at Anthea's beside it.

The data from Anthea's family tree was easier to enter. Once that was done, she transferred new information from the computer to her paper representations. Blue threads, yellow threads, some pink and purple even, but still red and green predominated. If she had Harry Jackson's father's details...

Anne Jackson's shadowy figure on the hospital veranda late at night…

No, she wasn't going to think about the Jacksons. What she needed was the Neil child—he was the only one about whom she had nothing. She'd visit Granny, see what she knew, then tomorrow she'd go out and visit the Neils.

Mrs Neil might be the silent type, but she wasn't frightening in any way. In fact, she was, if what Caitlin had heard was right, more likely to be frightened. Ezra Neil evoked fear in strangers who barely knew him—did his wife also fear him?

Realising she'd probably never know the answer, Caitlin banished thoughts of Ezra from her mind. With any luck, he'd be preaching somewhere in town in the morning and Mrs Neil would be on her own.

Caitlin reached the door then remembered the new lock. If the keys hadn't been sitting beside it, would she have remembered to either take or hide her laptop?

The realisation that she wouldn't have made her stomach squirm.

She picked it up, slid it into a plastic bag, put her notes and Anthea's family tree in with it, dithered over the patient files she had and in the end decided to take them, too, then carted it all over to the hospital.

Granny was looking well, sitting up in bed, her cheeks as pink as the knitted bed-jacket she was wearing.

'About time you visited again,' she scolded, and Caitlin apologised, explaining she'd wanted to get a lot of things sorted out before she came.

She opened up her representation of the families, and spread it on Granny's table, explaining who the people were and how they were connected.

Granny crowed with delight as her gnarled forefinger traced relationships.

'Bet Martha Stubbings—that's Anthea's mother—wouldn't want to know she's so closely related to the Wetherbys,' she remarked, jabbing her finger on a particular intersection of the map. 'Though the Wetherbys are good people, Martha's grandmother married a man on the land—the squattocracy, we call them out here. Martha's always made out her ancestors came straight from England and not on convict ships, but there's Wetherby blood there, too.'

Granny was obviously delighted by this bit of old history that had slipped her by. So much so, Caitlin hoped the old lady wouldn't run into Martha Stubbings any time soon.

'You've a lot of children at the bottom down here with red and green lines in them,' Granny pointed out to her, 'but they've all got other colours as well.'

'I know,' Caitlin told her, 'and there are so many of them, I really need at least one more connection to narrow down the selection.'

She hesitated, thinking again of her computer and the shadowy figure on the hospital veranda, certain Anne Jackson couldn't have caused the damage, yet aware she was the one person with a secret to keep.

Would Granny know the answer to that secret?

Was it fair to ask?

If children's lives might later benefit, then, yes.

'Taking you a while to decide something, isn't it?' Granny said, and Caitlin smiled at her perception.

'Do you know who Harry Jackson's father is?'

There, the question was out.

'No!'

'You didn't even stop and think,' Caitlin protested.

'I've been thinking for what—eight years? Nine? How old is the boy?'

'He's nine,' Caitlin confirmed.

'Well, that's how long no one's known and, believe me, keeping a secret like that in a town this small is no mean feat. Most people assume he was someone Anne met down in the city where she did her training because she was pregnant when she came home, but I've an idea he was local—someone she couldn't name.'

Granny lay back against her pillows and Caitlin realised the colour had leached from the elderly woman's cheeks.

'I'm sorry. I've tired you,' she said, folding up the paper.

'No,' Granny told her, placing her cold, bony hand on Caitlin's. 'Just a ghost walking over my grave.'

She closed her eyes.

'I'll be that ghost before long, I reckon,' she added quietly, and Caitlin, with a rush of affection for this woman she barely knew, leant forward and kissed her on the cheek.

'No way!' she said. 'You've got to stick around to see how things work out.'

Granny opened her eyes.

'You're the one who has to stick around,' she said. 'It's OK for old people like me to get sick and die, but children? Before they've had a chance at life? You keep looking, girl, and fighting those who try to stop you. Do you think this harsh outback land would ever have been settled if it weren't for the women who stuck it out, believing it would provide a better life for their children? That's what you're doing, girl, seeking a better life for everyone's children.'

She closed her eyes again, which gave Caitlin the opportunity to wipe some moisture from her own eyes.

'Thank you, Granny,' she whispered, then she kissed the wrinkled cheek again and quietly left the room.

Without asking about the Neils, she realised as she walked along the corridor towards the kitchen and the back door.

Nellie had been here forty years—maybe Nellie would know.

But Nellie was off duty, a woman Caitlin hadn't met reigning in her place in the kitchen.

The Neils would have to wait until tomorrow.

Back in her house, Caitlin dropped the bulging plastic bag on a chair and wondered what people at the golf club would think of it as a fashion accessory.

Golf club—Connor. Would he be there?

Which question led immediately to another. How should she behave if he was?

No answer, so she showered, carrying the bag into the bathroom with her and making do with lukewarm water in case steam affected computers.

Another question—the predictable dilemma of what to wear.

She decided on jeans and her favourite white linen shirt—dressing for comfort and the confidence being comfortable brought.

Hair up or hair down?

Connor's not going to be there, she reminded herself as she twitched and dithered, going for hair up and fiddling with eye-liner—something she rarely wore because she was so bad at applying it.

Tonight, however, it worked, and she looked at the stranger in the mirror, seeing eyes made larger and darker by the black outline.

She was immediately assailed by doubts that she'd overdone it, but a car was pulling up outside and it was too late to start again.

She switched off the light, found the key, picked up her precious plastic bag and headed out the door.

'Bringing your own dinner?' Mike asked, holding the car door open for her.

'No, my notes and laptop. Even with a new lock, I'm not leaving anything behind.'

'I'll lock it in the boot,' Mike said, reaching out to take the bag from her.

Caitlin hesitated, then reluctantly passed it over.

'No one will know it's there,' he added, but uneasiness at being parted from it made her look around, seeking a watcher on the back veranda of the hospital or someone lurking near one of the outbuildings.

'Anyway,' Mike said, as they drove out, 'I imagine whoever wrecked your computer thinks they've destroyed your work and that's an end to it.'

'You think that's what they were doing—destroying my work?'

Mike glanced her way.

'Of course—what else would it be?'

'I thought a warning,' Caitlin answered hesitantly, as a whole new scenario built up in her head.

'No,' she said, as Mike pulled up outside a low-set brick building. 'They didn't look for disks or destroy the paper files that were in a folder under the table. Surely if they wanted to destroy my work, they'd have taken everything.'

Mike raised his hand in a 'don't know' gesture.

'Who can say what the person was thinking?' he said, opening his car door and getting out, then coming around to Caitlin's side.

She got out herself, in time to hear him say almost under his breath, 'Particularly a person wielding an axe.'

'An axe? Someone hit my computer with an axe?'

Mike turned towards her, a frown drawing his sandy brows together.

'I thought you'd seen it.'

'Seen what?' a lighter voice demanded, and Caitlin looked up to see Sue and Connor, backlit by the light inside the clubhouse.

'Caitlin didn't realise whoever wrecked her computer used an axe,' Mike explained.

That drew an exclamation of annoyance from Connor and from Sue a disgusted, 'And I suppose you just told her and have now frightened the poor thing out of her wits.'

Connor, meanwhile, had stepped around Mike, stopping

next to Caitlin and putting his hand tentatively on her shoulder.

'It doesn't matter what the idiot used,' he said. 'Now, let's forget about it, and go inside for a drink. Sue and I have been abstaining until you arrived, although Sue won the "nearest the pin" and has been dying to celebrate.'

Caitlin glanced up into his face as he ushered them all inside, but it was blank—shuttered against her.

Unfortunately, her body still failed to realise it could no longer be attracted to his, and was telling her in count-less ways just what it thought of this proximity, while her mind was such a swamp of dismay and disbelief—an axe, for goodness' sake—she was tempted to give in to Connor's demands and leave town.

She didn't—not right then. In fact, she let herself be guided by Connor to a chair, then sat in it, tense and twitchy—worse when Connor took the chair beside her, with Mike and Sue across the table from them.

'So, tell me how it's going,' Sue demanded, while Mike went off to fetch drinks.

'Not here, Sue.' Connor answered before Caitlin had a chance to speak. 'In fact, the less said about Caitlin's re-search, here or anywhere in town, the better.'

'Oh!' Sue looked as surprised as she sounded, but, though Caitlin was equally surprised, she was also an-gered.

'That's ridiculous, Connor. You can't hide what I'm doing here. Anyone who doesn't already know just isn't interested. What's more, not talking about something doesn't make it go away.'

'And don't I know it!' he said bitterly, and Caitlin sensed he wasn't thinking about the research. Sensed also that the gulf between them was widening to such an extent it would never be bridged, and regrets for what might have been between them threatened to swamp her.

'So, how *is* it going?' Sue asked again, ignoring

Connor's ban and taking Caitlin's words as permission to discuss the research.

'Promising,' Caitlin replied, 'but I can't go further than that at the moment. I have a couple of things to follow up and should be able to do that tomorrow, then I have to collate what I have in order to see where to go next.'

She smiled at Sue.

'After that, who knows? I may have to return to Brisbane and find another theory to test.'

'But if you find the threads you need—find some links between the children—what then?'

'Then someone will take blood samples, run DNA tests and look for differences and similarities.' She hesitated, glanced at Connor, who was studying his drink as if analysing its molecules, then added, 'I'd like that someone to be me. I'd like the opportunity to follow through, which was the original intention. Finding genetic links is only the beginning, and in the end the theory could still lead to a dead end, but it would be my dead end.'

Connor gave an explosive snort.

'Can't you just say failure—say you're likely to fail—not use emotive language like "dead end"?'

He stood up and stormed away, Mike and Sue staring after him, Caitlin awash with guilt and regret. How could she have been so insensitive? Not thought first about her phrasing?

He was thinking of Angie, of course. Thinking of the woman he had loved.

The woman who was dead.

'What's eating him?' Mike asked, turning to his wife for an explanation.

'I've no idea. He played well so it can't be his golf.'

'Perhaps I'd better go,' Caitlin suggested. 'After all, this is your usual night out, and I'm the one upsetting him.'

'Don't you dare go,' Sue warned her. 'He's a grown man. He'll get over whatever it is that's upsetting him.'

But would he? Caitlin wondered.

Would he ever get over Angie?

The thought that he might not brought sadness to mix with the guilt, and she closed her eyes, wondering how a simple meal at the local golf club could have gone so wrong so quickly.

Connor walked out of the clubhouse and down across the darkened fairways, unaware of where he was going, knowing only he had to walk off some of the tension that simmered in his body, like molten metal in a cauldron, ready to flare out, burning anyone unwary enough to come close.

He'd been OK until Caitlin had walked into the clubhouse, blonde hair piled up on her head, revealing the long line of her neck, while wispy tendrils framed her delicate features. She was wearing blue jeans and a white shirt, not the most seductive or alluring clothes in the world, yet his body had ached with a fierce need and it had taken all his resolve not to go to her and take her in his arms— kiss her and claim her as his own, in front of most of the golf club members and any number of local drinkers who were propping up the bar.

But she wasn't his, and he doubted she would ever be because, irrational though it might be, deep down in his gut he knew the only way to keep her safe was to get her out of town. And for that, she'd hate him.

The thought caused him physical pain, but he turned back towards the clubhouse. He'd apologise, then spend the evening with his friends. He'd talk and laugh and act as close to normal as he possibly could. Then tomorrow he'd offer to help her finish this initial stage of her work— accompany her as she tied up the loose ends.

Mike saw him first and raised a hand in greeting, causing Caitlin to turn. Connor saw her eyes widen and a faint flush rise in her cheeks.

He closed the distance between them in two strides, and leant on the back of the chair he'd vacated earlier.

'If I apologise most humbly for my behaviour, will you let me join you?'

He was looking at the three of them but guessed Caitlin would know he was speaking to her.

'It's me who should apologise,' she said quietly, and reached out and rested her hand on his. 'Come on, sit down and join us.'

The touch sent fire spiralling through Connor's blood, and the look in Caitlin's eyes spread the heat along his nerves so desire now raged within him.

He sat, aware the proximity would make matters worse, but with that renewed surge of lust came a momentous idea.

They were two mature, consenting adults, who had—only last night?—agreed to explore the attraction that had flared between them.

What better way to keep Caitlin safe than to spend the night in bed with her? Not platonically, as he'd stupidly suggested the previous evening, but playfully, healthily and pleasurably.

He turned and smiled at her.

'Forgive me for losing it?' he asked quietly, while Mike and Sue debated what they'd eat.

She smiled and touched his arm, high-wattage electricity surging through him.

'I think I'm the one who should be asking that,' she murmured. 'It was thoughtless of me, Connor. I'm sorry.'

She looked so genuinely upset he shifted his hand beneath the table to touch her denim-clad thigh, giving it a little consoling squeeze. Then his hand felt so comfortable there he let it linger, and the thigh didn't move away, neither did its owner slap his face.

Both, he decided, extremely good signs...

They ordered their meal and Mike asked about the golf game. Sue teased him by saying she preferred Connor as a partner because he didn't tell her what she was doing wrong every time she played a stroke, but Mike countered by reminding her she usually won when she played with him, and he hadn't noticed her name being called out in the afternoon trophy list.

'Apart from nearest the pin,' she retorted.

The amiable bickering defused the last of the tension— well, one kind of tension, Caitlin decided. The other tension she was feeling had nothing to do with Connor's outburst earlier, but everything to do with the man himself.

While her body delighted in the warm hand resting, oh, so casually against her thigh, debate raged in her head.

It's only sexual!

So what's wrong with that?

Plenty, when you're the kind of woman who doesn't go for quick sexual flings.

Perhaps now's the time to start.

Nonsense!

Sue interrupted with a question about Granny, but Connor fielded it and Caitlin returned to the mental argument.

Why not?

Ah, no quick answer.

No slow answer either, she admitted to the demanding voice, but she suspected it might have something to do with the fact she felt more than pure sexual attraction towards Connor Clarke.

'When will you release her?'

Sue again, presumably still discussing Granny.

But if it's not sexual attraction, what is it?

She heard a scoffing laugh echoing in her head. Don't even think of love, it said. Not when the man concerned is still tied to a woman from his past.

CHAPTER TEN

THEIR meals arrived, and conversation turned to food, then drifted to books, took in the weather—invariably included in any talk in the country—and somehow reached a debate on the importance of sport in the nation's lifestyle.

'I don't mind watching sport on television,' Caitlin said, deciding she should contribute something because she'd spent most of the meal thinking about Connor and wondering just where things stood between them.

'Couch potato,' Connor teased.

He'd finished eating and his left hand had once again found its way to her thigh, where it was generating warmth throughout her body.

'Talking of couches,' Sue said, 'I'm nearly ready for bed. It must be the fresh air and exercise that makes me so tired on golf days—I'm sure it's more tiring than chasing the kids day in and day out.'

'If you find golf too tiring, I'll take over your day,' Mike offered, and got an elbow in the ribs from his wife.

'OK,' he added, 'I get the message. I'll take you home.'

He looked at Caitlin but before she could say anything, Connor spoke.

'I'll take Caitlin,' he said.

The fingers on her thigh exerted a little extra pressure. and he glanced her way, as if seeking her agreement.

Mouth dry with newly generated excitement, she nodded. Enough debating, her head said firmly. Just go with the flow.

The flow had her waiting at the table while Connor paid the bill, then they walked out into the car park, their fingers entwined, silence between them as if there was nothing that needed to be said.

Connor opened the car door and held it for her, releasing her hand only when the time came to close the door. He walked around the hood and climbed in beside her, turning to run his knuckles slowly down her cheek, as he'd done once before.

But this time the touch was a promise and the excitement Caitlin had been feeling deepened, so desire became a hunger and the option of turning back no longer existed.

Back at the house, they walked quietly up the steps, but once inside Connor's control broke. He uttered a hoarse exclamation and took her in his arms, kissing her with a burning intensity that would have frightened her if her own passion hadn't matched it.

Tenderness took flight and finesse went out the window as the pent-up emotion of the last twenty-four hours exploded between them. With shaking fingers they stripped off clothes, their own and each other's, fumbling clumsily, unaware of anything but the need to be naked.

'No!'

Connor's muttered word stopped the frenetic action, and Caitlin, shocked by how fast things had moved, needed the support of his hands on her arms to hold her steady.

He bent his head and kissed her, gently this time.

'Sorry,' he murmured softly, sliding his tongue across her upper lip. 'Things got a little out of hand just then, but I will not make love to you—not this first time—in the kitchen.'

Caitlin smiled and knew he'd felt her lips move against his when he gave her a quick hug, then swung her into his arms and carried her into a part of the house she'd never entered.

It was darker here than in the kitchen, then he turned into a room with wide doors open onto the veranda.

Moonlight flooded in, casting a silvery glow on a very large bed.

'Much better,' Connor said, setting her down then breathing heavily. 'That's if my gallantry in carrying you hasn't sapped all my energy.'

Caitlin linked her hands around his neck and drew him down on top of her.

'I don't think it has,' she whispered, then she kissed him and there was no further need for conversation.

Eventually they slept, wrapped together, then, as the moon shifted and the room grew darker, Connor woke.

Caitlin's body was tucked against his.

Safe!

But even as his mind said the word, he remembered what he'd thought earlier—how he'd had the mad idea of bringing her back here and making love to her to keep her safe. Shame that he'd even thought such a thing rushed through him, and guilt hovered darkly in his mind, although he knew without a doubt he'd made love to Caitlin because of how he felt about her, not as a ruse to keep her from harm.

And she didn't know he'd thought the way he had, so no harm had been done, he told himself, yet the taint of his thinking lingered like a shadow on his memories of the pleasure they'd shared.

So many shadows, he thought as the woman beside him stirred, then settled back to sleep. Though he'd known, even when they'd parted, he'd no longer been in love with Angie, the shadow of her death still fell across his life. And now the attack on Caitlin's computer was casting a far darker shadow.

Who could be hurt by her enquiries? If he could answer that question, he might—

The explosion was so loud he thought it was his house and turned automatically to shield Caitlin with his body.

'Connor! What was it?'

She was trying to sit up, and now he could hear the

alarms ringing at the hospital. He shot out of bed, grabbing for the shorts he kept on a chair—ready for late-night emergencies.

'You stay right here,' he said to Caitlin, and he took off, thrusting his feet into his casual shoes, hopping to get them on, moving steadily through the house and down the steps, then running across the park towards the hospital.

The siren calling the volunteer fire crew to work echoed eerily through the night and he thought of the other men who'd be tumbling out of bed and stumbling into the nearest clothes.

Lights were on all over the hospital and movement indicated the nursing staff were calmly and quietly evacuating patients. Was someone over in the hostel wing, alerting those there? And where was the fire?

'It's out the back—in Matron's house.'

He hadn't asked the question, but Anne Jackson, wheeling Granny down the front ramp and across the car park to the assembly area, answered anyway.

Connor skirted the building, and saw flames licking along the wall of the old timber house, spreading fast and furiously from what remained of Caitlin's beautiful red car.

'I've checked the house, the lady doctor's not in there.' Geoff Page, the wardsman on duty, was playing a heavy fire-hose on the section of the hospital building nearest the house. 'I thought it was better to save the hospital than worry about the house.'

Connor nodded to him, fighting a gut-wrenching nausea brought on by the destruction and the fearful thought of what might have been.

He went through the kitchen, filled with smoke, but from outside, not within, and continued down the veranda of the hostel wing, where he was pleased to find an aide had already woken the seven occupants and was herding them along the veranda in the other direction, to the assembly point on that side of the building.

Anne met him as he walked into the hospital proper.

'Everyone's out, Connor,' she said. 'All of them OK. We had to release Warwick's leg from traction, but kept him in his bed. Mrs Rennie's in a wheelchair, with a drip stand so we could keep the drip running, and Granny's in her bed. Bert Cannaway and Pat Hobson both walked.'

'Do you know what happened?' Connor asked, and Anne shook her head.

'Just an explosion out the back—huge noise—everyone woke up. Geoff came in and said it was Caitlin's car. I didn't stop to look, just got everyone out. Then I rang Mike.'

'You did the right thing,' Connor said, thinking of where the fire was and the likelihood of it spreading. 'I'll just take a look out the back then check our patients.'

He was about to walk away when Mike came through the front door.

'I'm going to check out the back,' he told Mike. 'Anne will fill you in.'

Connor walked back to where flames had now engulfed the small house. The firemen had arrived and while two hoses were pumping water onto the flames, two more were making sure the hospital itself was too wet to catch light should a flaming ember hit it.

'How's your gas enclosure holding up?' Bill Reynolds, the man in charge of this shift of firefighters, asked.

'I'm checking it now,' Connor told him, leading the way to where, with Bill's advice and help, the hospital had recently built a fireproof shed to hold its supply of medical gases.

The outer brick skin was warm to the touch, but Connor knew the insulating layers within the bricks would be keeping the gas tanks at a safe temperature.

Assured that things were under control, and the hospital building relatively safe, he skirted back around the building to check on patients.

Caitlin was standing in a patch of shadow just beyond

the car park, the white of her shirt and the gleam of her golden hair identifying her to him.

He detoured that way and took her in his arms, holding her close for a moment.

'It's my house?' she said, her voice telling him she already knew the answer.

'Yes.'

What else was there to say?

'And my car?'

No emotion, just a deadness in her usually vibrant tones that hurt him more than tears would have done.

'The hospital insurance should cover it,' he told her, and she turned away, moving out of the circle of his arms.

'That's not the point, is it, Connor?' she said bleakly. 'You were right. By stubbornly staying on I put all the patients, staff and hostel people at risk. I should have gone.'

She walked away, not towards his house but to the cluster of nurses and patients.

Every cell in Connor's body urged him to follow her, but he knew he couldn't. He might only have five hospitalised patients at the moment, but all five of them would be traumatised to some degree by what had happened, and the elderly hostel-dwellers also deserved his attention.

The sun was up, shining with unnecessary brightness, before he left the hospital, after being assured there was no further risk of danger and having settled the occupants back inside. Setting up the weights for Warwick's leg had taken longest, but now everyone was settled, most of the patients sleeping.

Ned Withers had fixed crime tape—incongruous in a quiet country town—around the burnt-out vehicle and one look at the destruction made Connor's heart hurt for Caitlin. The door of the house was open, the living room a watery mess, but there was no sign of her laptop, luggage or clothing.

He made his way tiredly back to his place, regret that he hadn't been able to be with her eating at him. He'd seen her again briefly when she'd helped bring the patients back inside, then later she'd been sitting on Granny's bed, talking quietly to her and Mrs Rennie, who were now sharing a room. But then she'd left, with nothing more than a nod in his direction.

She wasn't at the house. He checked each room although an air of emptiness had been obvious from the moment he'd walked in. The note was on the kitchen table, missed as he'd hurried to the bedroom. Missed because his subconscious hadn't wanted to see it?

Dear Connor, it began—at least she'd called him 'dear'.

I'm leaving town. I'd say I'm sorry but that doesn't begin to cover how I feel—about you, the town, the trouble. I don't know what lies ahead, just know that you were right about me being here, and that I cannot stay any longer.

There was a space between the last word and her name, as if there were other things she might have put there. 'Love' perhaps?

Connor crumpled the note in his hand, then straightened it out, reread it and shook his head. It was an unmistakable goodbye, but he couldn't accept she'd left town, just like that. Without talking to him—or leaving a phone number or address where he could reach her when life returned to normal!

He phoned Mike to ask what he knew.

'Nothing, Connor. I saw her about an hour or so ago. She asked me for my car keys—then must have brought them back because they're here on my desk. I said how sorry I was about her car, but you know how it was. There wasn't really time for chatting. Now I've got reams of paperwork to complete. Just what I didn't need.'

Connor tried to make a sympathetic noise but concern for Caitlin overrode all other considerations.

She'd been devastated by the fire—more, he suspected, by the trouble her remaining in town had caused than by the loss of her car.

So she'd left town.

How?

The all-night garage out on the highway had rental cars. Was that why she'd wanted Mike's car keys? To drive out there and hire a car?

He phoned the garage but wasn't pleased to have his guess confirmed.

'One of the lads drove the rental back to the hospital so she could drop off the car she was in,' the man explained. 'Clive, it was, but he's gone off duty now, so I can't tell you where she was headed.'

OK, Connor thought, so he was right about the car, but was he right about her leaving town?

Immediately?

It didn't fit with the determined woman who'd been willing to lose her job—and a position he knew she'd fought hard to gain—for the sake of a theory that might or might not prove correct.

His anxiety was like an internal attack of pins and needles, and he wished he'd taken more notice of her work— of the things she'd told him.

Smelling smoke, on his body as well as wafting from the hospital, he headed for the bathroom, showered, dressed, then walked back across the park again.

Caitlin followed the directions the helpful fellow at the garage had given her, leaving the bitumen road for a gravel road that wound in and out between tall trees. The turn-off she was looking for was unmarked, the friendly man had said, but she'd know it by the way a tree had fallen across the track and cars now had to go around the tree.

'Not that many cars go out there—apart from Ezra's.'

Caitlin found the track, the tree across it so big that if she hadn't known about the detour around it, she'd have driven on, assuming it impassable. As she negotiated her way cautiously around the obstacle, she wondered about the sanity of what she was doing. Here she was, still in the clothes she'd worn to dinner at the golf club, reeking of smoke from the fire, tired almost beyond endurance, yet still pursuing the information that had already caused so much trouble in the town.

Her foot hovered over the brake, then she realised the track was too narrow, too hemmed in by trees, for her to turn the car. She'd *have* to drive on.

A couple of hundred metres further on there was a clearing, but now that she could turn around she didn't, knowing she had to finish what she had started. An ancient wooden house stood in the middle of the clearing, backed up against an assortment of sheds and strange-looking structures, like half-completed windmill towers.

As she stopped in front of the house, she remembered Ezra Neil was one of the men who still made a living mining gold. The towers must be connected to his mine or mines, she decided, though her knowledge of gold-mining was zilch.

Mrs Neil appeared as Caitlin got out of the car. The woman stood in the doorway of the house, not coming forward in welcome but not waving Caitlin away either. She just stood and looked at the visitor, making Caitlin feel distinctly uncomfortable.

'I would have phoned first but couldn't find a number,' Caitlin told her.

'We don't have the phone,' Mrs Neil replied.

Caitlin looked around. She'd heard so much about Ezra Neil and, although she'd never seen the man, she didn't like the idea that he might be lurking somewhere.

'I wondered if I could talk to you about my research,' she said, unwilling to approach the house without an invitation. 'About what I'm doing and what I hope to prove.'

'Talk won't bring Jonah back,' Mrs Neil told her, then she turned her head a fraction, as if someone in the kitchen had spoken to her. 'But you've come this far so you might as well come in.'

Caitlin wasn't sure whether to be pleased or sorry. It was a small victory, but she'd far rather have stayed outside the house where mellow sunshine would make mockery of strange fancies.

The kitchen, where she entered, was as spic and span as she would have expected Mrs Neil's kitchen to be, but bare and somehow soulless.

Another fancy the sunshine might have dispelled!

'Would you like a cup of tea?'

'No, thank you,' Caitlin said. 'I don't want to keep you long. It's just that Jonah's family is the only one that's missing from my research, and if I can get some details, I'll be finished and able to leave town.'

It was impossible to judge whether this information pleased Mrs Neil, as her face was as expressionless as ever.

'You'd better have some tea, then,' she said, and Caitlin, unwilling to refuse a second time, agreed.

'I'm trying to find out which children had the same bloodlines as the ones who got leukaemia,' she explained, as Mrs Neil went through the motions of fixing tea. 'Then I can look at those who didn't get it to see if there's any difference in their genetic structure that protected them.'

She was talking too much, and knew what she was saying was too technical, but the alternative was silence, and she couldn't have handled that either. Besides, she'd explained all this to the other mothers, why not to Mrs Neil?

'If we could find that out, we could protect children in the future.'

'There's no future once you're dead,' Mrs Neil decreed, and she turned back to face Caitlin with a small, but no less deadly looking gun in her hand.

'Now, leave your car keys on the table and walk back out the door,' Mrs Neil ordered. 'I didn't want to kill you. It causes too much talk. But you wouldn't listen, wouldn't go away.'

'Killing me won't help,' Caitlin said, thinking of Connor's Angie—knowing now how she'd died. Knowing now it wasn't Ezra she should have feared. 'Because someone else will come to finish my work. You can't just keep killing people.'

'Stand up and walk out.' Mrs Neil's voice was still as calm as it had been when she'd suggested a cup of tea, but Caitlin felt she must be feeling nervous.

Did nervous people shoot more readily?

Or might their hands shake so they'd miss?

Had Angie stood up when Mrs Neil had produced the gun? Had she thought if she was outside she could run?

Had she run and fallen down the shaft by accident, or been herded there by this madwoman?

It wasn't bravery, or fear of falling down a mine shaft, that kept Caitlin where she was. Given the choice of being shot in a spotlessly clean kitchen or falling down a mine shaft a snake could well have fallen down before her—it was no contest.

Guns were minor compared to snakes…

'I don't think so,' Caitlin said, when Mrs Neil repeated her order. 'If you're going to shoot me, you'll have to do it here, and that'll make an awful mess of your clean kitchen floor.'

She looked Mrs Neil directly in the eyes, and hoped she sounded calmer than she felt.

'And as well as that, there'll be the bullet in my body. You didn't shoot Angie so you got away with it that time, but a bullet can be traced to a gun. Of course, if the gun is your husband's, he'll probably get the blame.'

'Ezra wouldn't shoot anyone,' Mrs Neil proclaimed. 'Ezra's a saint.'

'Then he wouldn't want you shooting people, would he?' Caitlin asked, desperate to keep the woman talking and perhaps win herself a reprieve.

Any reprieve!

'Ezra doesn't know about the other one, and when you walk out of here, which you'll do eventually, my girl, he won't need to know about you either.'

Caitlin decided this was hopeful information, and confirmed her notion that Mrs Neil wouldn't shoot her in the house.

She thought of an old joke, about where did someone shoot you, in the foot, no, in the house, and had a totally inappropriate urge to smile.

Somehow, smiling in front of Mrs Neil seemed like a very bad idea.

Ezra Neil was standing out the back of the hospital, surveying what was left of Caitlin's car. In an instant, all the vague suspicions Connor had harboured against this man came to the fore, and he rushed forward, intending to grab him and demand to know why he'd done it.

And whether he'd killed Angie.

But Ezra turned to face him, and the sorrow in the man's face was so evident, the demands and accusations dried on Connor's lips.

'Where's the lady doctor?' Ezra asked.

'I don't know,' Connor said, still nursing the remnants of his suspicion. 'Do you?'

Ezra's eyes, deep-set and so dark as to be almost black, glimmered at him.

'The Lord looks after his own,' he said to Connor.

'I thought that was the devil,' Connor replied, and Ezra

shook his head, as if to remove himself from such flippancy.

'Why are you here, Ezra?' Connor asked, genuinely puzzled by the man's presence. And by the sense of pain emanating from him.

'My wife's missing.'

'Mrs Neil? Missing? How do you mean, missing?'

'Not at home—that's how I mean missing,' Ezra said. 'When I woke up this morning she wasn't there and the truck was gone. I walked to the main road and hitched into town but the truck's not here either.'

He rubbed his hand across his head in a gesture of such infinite weariness Connor felt a pang of pity for him.

But pity didn't stop him asking, 'Why would it be here?'

Ezra shrugged.

'She works here. When I heard about the fire—Jack Griffith gave me a lift and he knew—I thought maybe she'd heard too, I don't know how—nothing makes sense—but if she did hear, maybe she'd come in to help—'

He broke off, and Connor had the sense that the man didn't believe a word of his own explanation.

'How long ago did you leave your place?' he asked, and Ezra frowned as if he didn't understand the question.

'Mrs Neil might be home by now,' Connor explained.

'It was the boy getting ill like that,' Ezra said, as if carrying on a conversation Connor hadn't heard. 'She couldn't handle it—couldn't even go to Brisbane for his treatment. I took him down and stayed there. I was with him when he died. My wife…'

He stopped as if there was no way to explain, but he'd said enough to cause new concern to Connor.

'Ezra, when you came here, were you looking for the doctor or for your wife?'

The dark eyes met his.

'On my honour, Dr Clarke, until the new doctor came,

I didn't have even the faintest suspicion that my wife could do harm to someone. I am a man of God and, though I've sinned and done harm, I've tried to make amends and to live my life without harm to even the lowliest of His creatures. My wife—I thought my wife had followed the same path, but she was agitated when Dr Robinson was here and only calmed down when she disappeared. Then lately she's been strange again, talking to herself, then disappearing at odd times.'

Fear coagulated Connor's blood and he reached out and grabbed Ezra's shoulders and shook his thin frame.

'For God's sake, man, say what you mean. If you think the doctor is in danger from your wife, tell me. We'll find Mrs Neil, and take care of her. If she's sick, she'll get help.'

Ezra shook Connor off.

'I don't know what I mean, just what I fear. Drive me back to my place. If she did this, she will have gone home afterwards, probably thinking she'd be there before I woke. I walked across country to the highway and could have missed seeing the truck drive back.'

Connor hurried him back to the house where his car was parked.

'Why is she upset?' he asked Ezra as they sped out of town.

'With the other doctor, she was upset about the blood tests. She is a simple woman, and doesn't understand a lot of things, so all I can think is that she has some idea in her head that taking blood is bad.'

'But this doctor isn't talking about taking blood,' Connor protested, adding a silent, Not yet.

'But she's talking about families, and relationships. That would be enough.'

Enough for what? Connor wanted to scream at him, but the man was shaking with tension, so Connor concentrated on driving.

'Turn here,' Ezra said, and Connor turned, nearly hitting a huge tree that had fallen across the track.

He saw the detour and drove around it, then down the narrow lane until it widened out and he saw the house and outbuildings.

And a car!

'The truck's there,' Ezra said, pointing to a shed beyond the house.

'And the car?' Connor asked.

'I don't know,' Ezra replied, then he turned to Connor. 'I want you to stay here in the car. Let me go and speak to her.'

Ezra's eyes pleaded with him and though Connor's instincts shouted at him to find Caitlin—if she was here—he knew Ezra was right. If Mrs Neil was already unbalanced, seeing Connor might push her over the edge.

Ezra got out of the car and, although anyone in the house would have heard their approach, he didn't shut the door.

He was walking purposefully towards the house, calling to his wife, when the shot rang out, then Mrs Neil appeared in the doorway, a small black object in her hand.

Another shot and Ezra fell to the ground, then Mrs Neil screamed and ran towards him, the gun flying from her hand when she tripped and fell only feet from her fallen husband.

Connor flew out of the car and raced towards the house, sure someone had been injured by the first shot.

Praying it was injured, not dead.

Praying it wasn't Caitlin...

Caitlin was sitting on the floor under the table, her left hand clasped to her side, with her right elbow clamped against it—blood seeping through her fingers.

'Did you get the gun off her?' she asked, her voice so calm Connor found the words hard to understand.

'Caitlin—'

He came towards her, made to kneel, but she held up her hand.

'I'm all right. Find where she is, get the gun, or she'll kill us both, Connor.'

Her fingers were red with blood but he knew she was right, and he turned back to the door, peering cautiously out. Mrs Neil was kneeling beside Ezra, wailing loudly. The gun was on the ground where it had fallen and Connor left the house, hurrying across the grass, picking up the deadly weapon and pocketing it before crossing towards the fallen man.

'He's dead. Jerry's dead. Now everyone's dead,' Mrs Neil cried, but though Connor didn't know much about guns, he couldn't believe a small one could kill a man at such a distance.

'Let me look at him,' he said, but Mrs Neil flung herself across her husband's body.

'Jerry's mine, don't touch him,' she cried, and rather than argue he continued on to his car, pulled out his mobile and phoned for an ambulance and the police. Ned Withers was having a busy few days!

Then Connor lifted his bag from the back of the vehicle and hurried back to the house.

Inside, Caitlin had edged towards the wall and was leaning back on it, her cheeks as white as the shirt she was wearing.

'I've got the gun,' he said, squatting beside her, wanting desperately to take her in his arms and hold her tightly, but worried about the wound, the blood—her lungs. Dear heaven, had the bullet penetrated her lungs? Was she drowning in her own blood? He steadied himself and told her what she needed to know. 'Ezra's been shot but Mrs Neil won't let me near him, and I don't want to upset her more by forcing the issue. Now, let me look at your wound.'

He was trying to act normally but he could hear the tremor in his voice and the fingers reaching into his bag for a pressure pad were shaking so much he couldn't pick it up. He took a deep breath to calm himself, then touched her hand, lifting her fingers away and pressing the pad in their place. Blood prevented him seeing the extent of the damage, and for now stopping the bleeding was a priority.

'It hurts, Connor,' she said faintly, then she tried to smile and he thought his heart would break. 'It didn't hurt at first. She wanted me to go outside—but I was scared of snakes.'

Her eyelids fluttered closed, and a slight change in her breathing suggested her brain might have chosen to shut down rather than bear the pain.

He bandaged the pad into place, talking all the time, telling her how much he loved her, how she had to stay alive, get well.

'That's all that matters, Caitlin. We'll work things out from there. Just stay alive, my darling.'

Her breathing was steady, but that didn't stop terrible scenarios presenting themselves in his head, and fear that he'd lose the woman he loved so dearly reduced him to a stuttering mess.

The ambulance arrived, followed closely by Ned Withers, and Connor had to muster every last remnant of his self-control in order to leave Caitlin's side and go out to tend to Ezra. He kissed her gently on the cheek, still murmuring his love, and went outside. With the help of the two attendants, he managed to administer a sedative to Mrs Neil. Ned put her in the back of his vehicle, where she sat as if totally uninterested in the havoc she'd caused. Ezra was alive, but the bullet had hit him high up in the chest. Even as he was loaded into the ambulance, Connor knew he'd need to be airlifted out.

He was bandaging a pressure pad to the wound, anxious to stop further blood loss, when the ambulance attendants carried Caitlin out of the house. The fear that had fluttered in his chest since he'd realised she was missing, had settled into a lumpy kind of ache, and, looking at her pale face framed by the golden hair, he wondered how he would have survived if anything worse had happened to her.

Wondered how he'd survive when she went away—for what would keep a research scientist in a town like Turalla? Especially a research scientist who'd fled a small country town at sixteen!

CHAPTER ELEVEN

'LOVE?' Caitlin suggested, when Connor actually put this question to her a week later.

She was sitting in the sun on his veranda, her legs resting on a small table.

Smiling at him!

'Anyway,' she continued, 'I didn't think Turalla featured in your long-term plans.'

He settled on a chair in front of her, where he could see her face and rest his hand on her ankle—still needing both sight and touch to reassure himself she was alive.

'It didn't,' he said, trying to put into words some of the things that had passed through his mind during the traumatic days after the fire and the shootings. 'I was going to find out what had happened to Angie and leave.'

He hesitated, wondering how to explain and knowing, however the words came out, they were a signal that what had barely begun between them was about to end. Caitlin might talk of love, but her work was such a huge part of her life—

'Come on,' she prompted. 'You've been trying to work out how to say what you want to say for days—just spit it out.'

'I can't leave the town right now. This kind of thing doesn't just affect one family. It causes ripples right through the population.'

He sighed. 'When I first applied to come here, getting back to the city was always a priority, but now I don't know, Caitlin. I like working here, I like the people, and the lifestyle, and I also believe that country towns, however small, deserve a better deal with medical services.

Why shouldn't they have a local doctor who stays put, as your father did, instead of a series of young medicos intent on doing a year here then hightailing it out? Angie would have stayed, and although I'm not obligated in any way to take her place, I can't help feeling I could have a happy life here.'

Caitlin heard the commitment in his voice, but she also felt his love for her in the tender way he wrapped his fingers around her ankle. She knew there was more, and waited for it.

'Of course, things changed when you drove into town.' He thrust his free hand through his hair in the helpless gesture she'd grown to love. 'Now I'm reasonably sure I wouldn't have a happy life anywhere you weren't, so staying here for ever doesn't seem to be an option.'

'Not even if I stayed, too?' she asked, and saw his eyes widen, then a frown draw his brows together as if he couldn't understand the words.

'But why? Your work! It's too important to you. You—'

The protests might have continued forever if Caitlin hadn't interrupted, leaning forward and capturing the hand that had been toying with her ankle.

'Didn't you hear what I said earlier?' she asked him. 'I know the question about what would keep me here was hypothetical, but my answer wasn't. Love would keep me here, Connor. If you wanted me to stay…'

'If I wanted you to stay? Of course I'd want you to stay, but that's not fair on you.'

With an effort that caused exquisite pain in her damaged floating ribs, she leaned further forward and rested her hand against his cheek.

'Connor, I can work from here. Even after I finish what I'm doing at the moment, with a computer link to the lab I can continue doing analysis, which is mainly what I do anyway.'

'Here? In Turalla? You mean you'd stay?'

Caitlin chuckled.

'For an intelligent man, you take a bit of getting through to! I know I've only been here a couple of weeks, but it's been a revelation, coming back to a country town. I didn't realise how much I missed the sense of community.'

Connor clasped her hand in his, holding it pressed against his cheek.

'I love you, Caitlin,' he said quietly, and she felt the warmth of his affection swamp her body.

'Hey, stop snogging on the veranda, you two. It sets a bad example for the youngsters.'

Mike stood below them, his four children chasing each other around him, the twins using his legs as an escape tunnel.

'I'll throw the surgery keys down to you,' Connor said. 'Grab the box of blocks out of the waiting room and come on up. I'll shout you a cup of coffee and you can tell us what's happening while the kids play with the blocks.'

It took a while to organise, but eventually Mike was settled in a chair beside them.

'I've just had a call from Anne. Ezra's out of danger, and should be well enough to be flown back next week.'

Connor shook his head.

'I still can't believe the Anne part of the puzzle,' he said, 'even though I was there when she came up to the hospital before he was airlifted out and actually saw her reaction to his injury.'

'Sue's pieced it all together, and when I spoke to Anne she filled in the blanks,' Mike said. 'Sue and Anne both trained in Brisbane, living in at the nurses' quarters. And although Anne was older, Sue remembers seeing Ezra around the place. That's one part. Then, Connor, you said Mrs Neil kept calling Ezra Jerry. After she shot him.'

'Jerry was Ezra's brother,' Caitlin offered, remembering someone telling her about the two boys.

'Exactly!' Mike said. 'Apparently he left home while

still a youngster, and led a wild life. Ezra was always the good son, and he went off to Brisbane to university—he was doing religious studies so he must always have wanted to be a preacher. He met up with Anne and they began an affair. He had no idea what had happened to Jerry until Mrs Neil—whose name, by the way, is Candace, would you believe—came to him to tell him Jerry had been killed in a bikie fight and she was pregnant with Jerry's baby. Ezra, who because of his religious beliefs was already riddled with guilt about his affair, did what he thought was the right thing—broke it off with Anne and married Candace.'

'Oh, for heaven's sake!' Caitlin spluttered. 'How do people make such a *mess* of their lives? I assume Anne then found out she was pregnant, and Harry is Ezra's child.'

She thought for a moment, then said, 'Oh!' And covered her mouth with her hand.

Connor smiled. 'I bet you're thinking this is good for your research,' he said, and she had to agree that it might just provide the extra links she needed.

But she forgot about the research when Connor added, 'I think Rachel could be Ezra's child as well. Ezra told me he took Jonah down to Brisbane. If Anne was there with Harry at the same time, it's only logical the two of them would have shared just a little comfort.'

'Oh, dear, how sad it all is,' Caitlin murmured, thinking how terrible it would be to have to hide one's love. Especially when the loved one lived in the same small town!

'But why did Angie have to die?' Connor asked Mike. 'Did Sue work that out, too?'

'No, but Ned Withers did. Mrs Neil—no way I can even *think* of her as Candace—won't be judged fit to stand trial, but she's told Ned enough for him to work out what had happened. She isn't very bright, but one thing that she seemed to know was that blood tests could prove paternity. She didn't know how or why—or that it would take a specific request—but had it in her head that if Angie took blood from Ezra a sign would flash across the blood bank computer saying, This man is not Jonah's father. And it was important to her that no one knew that.'

'Her respectability was important to her,' Connor said quietly, and Caitlin reached out and took his hand, knowing he was thinking of Angie, and how she'd died for such a stupid reason.

'I suppose some good's come out of it all,' Mike said. 'Ezra and Anne can eventually get together.' He looked out over the veranda railing as if seeing into the future. 'And maybe you two as well.'

'Maybe,' Caitlin echoed, turning to Connor with a teasing smile.

'Definitely maybe,' Connor said. 'Or should that be maybe definitely?'

He turned to Mike.

'Actually, if you'd remove yourself and your brood from the vicinity, I could continue what I was doing before you interrupted. Not snogging, as you so indelicately put it, but persuading this woman to turn a maybe into a yes.'

'I'm out of here,' Mike said, standing up and calling to his children. They came scampering around the corner, and he lifted the twins, one on each arm. 'I only came to say Sue has spread the word. The hospital's Sunday barbecue is at our place tonight.'

He walked towards the steps then turned back to say, 'Maybe you'll have an announcement to make. Something we can all drink to—a toast to the future!'

Connor walked to the steps with him and watched as he returned to his car, then he came back and this time pulled his chair so it was beside Caitlin's.

'Will we have an announcement to make?' he asked, and she looked into his eyes, seeing not the blue-green colour but the love he felt for her.

'Soon,' she said. 'But for now let's keep it to ourselves. Let's enjoy getting to know each other better, and just being together, before announcing anything and having the whole town intrude on our relationship.'

Connor leaned over and kissed her on the lips.

'You've been away from country towns too long,' he told her, 'if you think it takes an announcement for the town to intrude. Just yesterday Mrs Rennie's daughter brought me an embroidered towel kind of thingy her mother had made as an engagement present.'

'Oh!' Caitlin said, then she kissed him back, because if the town was about to intrude she had to make the most of every moment she had alone with this man!

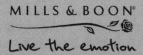

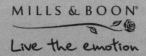

A *Mother's Day Gift*

A collection of brand-new romances just for you!

Margaret Way

Anne Ashley

Lucy Monroe

On sale 5th March 2004

Available at most branches of WHSmith, Tesco, Martins, Borders, Eason, Sainsbury's and all good paperback bookshops.

FREE!

4 Books
and a surprise gift!

We would like to take this opportunity to thank you for reading this Mills & Boon® book by offering you the chance to take FOUR more specially selected titles from the Medical Romance™ series absolutely FREE! We're also making this offer to introduce you to the benefits of the Reader Service™—

- ★ FREE home delivery
- ★ FREE gifts and competitions
- ★ FREE monthly Newsletter
- ★ Books available before they're in the shops
- ★ Exclusive Reader Service discount

Accepting these FREE books and gift places you under no obligation to buy; you may cancel at any time, even after receiving your free shipment. Simply complete your details below and return the entire page to the address below. *You don't even need a stamp!*

YES! Please send me 4 free Medical Romance books and a surprise gift. I understand that unless you hear from me, I will receive 6 superb new titles every month for just £2.60 each, postage and packing free. I am under no obligation to purchase any books and may cancel my subscription at any time. The free books and gift will be mine to keep in any case.

M4ZEE

Ms/Mrs/Miss/Mr ....Initials ....
BLOCK CAPITALS PLEASE

Surname ....

Address ....

....

....Postcode ....

Send this whole page to:
UK: The Reader Service, FREEPOST CN8I, Croydon, CR9 3WZ
EIRE: The Reader Service, PO Box 4546, Kilcock, County Kildare (stamp required)

Offer not valid to current Reader Service subscribers to this series. We reserve the right to refuse an application and applicants must be aged 18 years or over. Only one application per household. Terms and prices subject to change without notice. Offer expires 30th May 2004. As a result of this application, you may receive offers from Harlequin Mills & Boon and other carefully selected companies. If you would prefer not to share in this opportunity please write to The Data Manager at the address above.

Mills & Boon® is a registered trademark owned by Harlequin Mills & Boon Limited.
Medical Romance™ is being used as a trademark.
The Reader Service™ is being used as a trademark.